Joseph Palmer, Cynthia Morgan St. John

A Fortnight's Ramble to the Lakes in Westmorland, Lancashire, and

Cumberland

Joseph Palmer, Cynthia Morgan St. John

A Fortnight's Ramble to the Lakes in Westmorland, Lancashire, and Cumberland

ISBN/EAN: 9783337780760

Printed in Europe, USA, Canada, Australia, Japan

Cover: Foto ©Andreas Hilbeck / pixelio.de

More available books at **www.hansebooks.com**

A FORTNIGHT'S RAMBLE

TO

THE LAKES

IN

WESTMORELAND, LANCASHIRE,

AND

CUMBERLAND.

BY A RAMBLER.

HEAVENS! what a goodly profpect fpreads around
Of Hills, and Dales, and Woods, and Lawns ! ——
— — — — — — — —
— — — — — — — —

Happy BRITANNIA ! where the QUEEN OF ARTS
Infpiring vigour, Liberty abroad
Walks, unconfin'd, even to thy fartheft cots,
And fcatters plenty with unfparing hand.

THOMSON.

THE SECOND EDITION.

REFERENCES.

Fell,	a barren mountain.
Crag,	a rough-topped hill.
Syke,	a little rivulet.
Tarn,	a small lake.

An Explanation of some of the Provincial Words.

an,	—	have.
aw,	—	all.
bu,	—	but.
con,	—	can.
cum,	—	come.
deed,	—	died.
dun naw,	—	do not.
faither,	—	father.
feact,	—	fact.
fealt no pean,		felt no pain.
fellar,	—	fellow.
gien um feck,		given them such.
lard,	—	lord.
neames,	—	names.
tha mun,	—	thou must.
th' cradle,	—	the cradle.
thinken umselves,		think themselves.
t' kno,	—	to know.
um,	—	them.
wad,	—	would.
yon mon,	—	yonder man.

N. B. As the Author has no Vocabulary to go by, he judges from the ear.

To Mr. WILLIAM NOBLE,
of LONDON.

WERE there a man on earth whom I efteem more than I do you, to him fhould this book have been dedicated. You expreffed a wifh to vifit your native country. Moft willingly I accompanied you. A better guide I could not have had. Your approval of my defcriptions made me write with energy and fleetnefs, and drew me before the publick.

To

To make known the many obligations I am under to you, would hurt your feelings, and I could not do juftice to the fubject. One amongft the leaft I venture to fpeak of.— You ordered a captain of a fhip, during hard times at Gibraltar, to fupply me with whatever I wanted, cither in meat, liquors, or apparel.

I will fay no more; but in this little I mean every thing that is grateful; and, am with real efteem,

My dear friend,

your very obliged,

and faithful fervant,

Sloane-Street,
May 23, 1795.   JOS. BUDWORTH.

PREFACE.

LOUNGING away my time at my bookseller's, a North country gentleman came into the shop, and enquired for *A Fortnight's Ramble*. Unfortunately this man of decision opened the book where Fancy had been ranging. I never shall forget the twist with which he threw it down, saying—" this man pretends to be a

a 4 " wit;

" wit; I'll purchafe none of it." My bookfeller and I interchanged a fmile at this new order of criticifm ;- and, if this edition fhould fall into my cenfor's hands, I hope he will read thus far; as I would wifh to remind him of the full inveftigation of the facts on which he grounded his ver-dict.

The fale of the firft edition was larger than I had any right to ex-pect; and it would have been more fo, had I not been convinced it was very incorrect: I owed it therefore to the publick, to difregard emolu-ment, and it has been two years fuppreffed.

It

It paffed not through the literary ordeal without experiencing a feverity of criticifm, that has been of fervice to me; and amongft thofe Reviewers who had made the tour. I feel gratified in having been allowed " to prefent fcenes afrefh to the memory"—and anfwering for— " fidelity in defcription."

Much as I wifhed the former book to have undergone the improvement of correction; I knew not how to afk any one to trouble himfelf with fo unwelcome an employ—efpecially as a literary perfon, whofe early purfuits in life were the fame as my own, had declined a fimilar requeft, from a multiplicity of

pub-

public and more interefting engage-
ments; but, when " the tempeft of
politicks" engroffes the mind, rural
fcenes can only tend to encreafe
mental turbulence, by a momentary
reflection on the quiet it has forfaken;
and who would envy the fame and
fortune of any one in poffeffion of
both, by mixing in troubled waters?

I have now the good fortune to
acknowledge obligations to the Rev.
Mr. Holme, vicar of Shap in Weftmoreland, who has not only cor-
rected many errors fo volatile a
writer is liable to, but hath favoured me with interefting notes.—
Although unknown to this clergyman,
I have reafon to think with thofe
who fpeak of him, that he is a man

of

of eminent abilities; and it is probably a lofs to the learned world,
that fo good a fcholar has been fo
long concealed under fo fmall a living—

> " To all the country dear,
> " And paffing rich on forty pounds a year."

By fuch affiftance I with more confidence meet " the wrinkled brow."

My memory has prefented me
with additions both in profe and
verfe; and I make no apology for
introducing a village-wedding to the
notice of thofe who can be charmed with partial cuftoms in country
life.

This excurfion was at the requeft
of a friend; and I was fo pleafed

2   with

with every thing I faw, I hope there are fome few who will not be difpleafed with my manner of telling it. Whatever I have written, came warm from the imagination, with the views full before it. I have always been an admirer of the works of Nature, and I never faw them in fuch liberal features before: I have no fine houfes, no fine paintings, no compliments to great people, to fwell out my book with;— my portraits are cottagers, my pictures what Nature has lavifhed around them.—When I do praife a rich man, it fhall never be on account of his wealth, but for thofe unremitting acts of philanthropy, thofe only deferving of efteem, that

fhower

fhower down in charity wherever it is wanted,

The inhabitants are as peaceful as their valleys, and feem to have no inclination to leave them : they even talk of their forefathers, and carry an oral account for feveral generations of any one who has been out of the common way. One man told us, " My faither, gran-
" faither, an grait granfaither,
" fearmed yon lake, an I wad naw
" leave this pleace for aw th'
" world."—This valley had no more than fourteen houfes, and is fo entombed in mountains, that only one chaife has been known to vifit it.——Happy man ! well doft thou prove that Nature impreffes the

the ftrongeft attachments where fhe is undifturbed, and that every thing around them grows in their minds, and becomes a neceffary part of them.——Pr'ythee, Mortal! doft not thou think this fimple villager has given (in a few words) as practical a proof of contentment as volumes could contain?

Thofe who make the tour of the Lakes, and will examine any of the views I attempt to defcribe, if they fee them from the points I did, and in the laft week in July and the firft in Auguft, making allowances for the fancies of Nature, or the pruning hand of man, may, perhaps, give me the credit of delineating faithfully; and they will be well repaid

repaid, againſt any of my omiſſions, by finding out new beauties of their own: and I truſt thoſe who do not viſit them, by taking the trouble of peruſing this Ramble, will have ſome enlivening ſcenes and uſeful characters preſented to them.

We were exactly one fortnight, with conſtant fine weather *, during which we walked upwards of two hundred and forty miles, beſides boat and chaiſe conveyance; and what with admiring the wonders around us, writing them down, or ſtoring them in my memory for an

* We commenced our Ramble after very wet weather, which gave us a ſight of the waterfalls to advantage; the day we finiſhed it began to rain— and I believe a wetter Autumn was never known.

early

early morning's pen, I can truly
fay, I enjoyed a noble hurry of imagination, and that I had not time
to be idle.

The friend I accompanied was
my guide; he had been at the
Lakes before: his tafte led him thi-
ther again, and I have to exprefs
myfelf fingularly obliged for many
features he pointed out, which my
mind had not taken in. He had
" Mr. WEST's Guide to the Lakes,"
but did not make ufe of it. Mr.
WEST, I underftand was a fcholar
of a warm fancy; he had ftudied
their beauties minutely, and, from
living near them, took time to be
correct. I believe that gentleman
has brought much company, and

4   will

will always be recollected (for he is now no more!) as their beſt patron. I would with pleaſure have read his book, if I had not been apprehenſive it might have ſuppreſſed this, which does not merit the name of a Guide, and is only offered as a Journeying Companion. It was cuſtomary, I am told, to daſh by them with an exclamation or two of, " Oh! how fine!" &c.; or, as a gentleman ſaid to Robin Partridge the day after we were upon Windermere, " Good God! " how delightful!—how charming! " —I could live here for ever!— " Row on, row on, row on, row on ;" and after paſſing one hour of exclamations upon the Lake, and half an hour at Ambleſide, he ordered his horſes into his phaëton, and flew off

b   to

to take (I doubt not) an equally-flying view of Derwentwater. Robin Partridge, when he told us of it, afked us if we thought " the gentleman " was as compofed as he fud be?"

It is now fo meritoriouſly the faſhion to make this tour, I dare almoſt fay it will be thought want of taſte not to be able to fpeak about it; for, it only wants to be made, to have the preference of every fummer excurſion in the kingdom. Had thefe beauties been formed in a foreign land, they would have been long ago more known ; but ſince a once-boaſted, though now unfortunate, part of the Continent is become a fcene of horror and devaſtation, they may be thought worthy

thy attention.—I was telling a Grand Tourift where I had been; and he dafhed off to Switzerland. We have no reafon to depreciate other countries in commending our own; but Nature has fported fuch variety AT HOME, no views can exceed them in that delightful miniature which the eye takes in, without being either glutted by expanfe, or DISGUSTED by deformity.

The fhortnefs of our Ramble did not allow us to vifit every Lake; and I regret what I have faid of Baffenthwaite, Coniftone, and Hawfwater, is fo unequal to what they merit—we only faw them in perfpective. I ftill hope to vifit them, for, in my rambling life, I have never

b 2   feen

feen any thing equal to their beauties; and to repeat the pleafures I enjoyed is a moft refrefhing fatisfaction, and I muft think it *allowed*
tautology.—Amblefide, or Low
Wood, are the beft fituated for head-
quarters the firft week; and Kefwick,
for the remainder of the tour. Kefwick is the little London of the towns
about the Lakes; and we obferved,
as in all large places, the expence is
greater.

Reader! when thou confidereft
the laborious mountains we traverfed,
with but *one arm* to truft to, and that
the greateft part of the writing took
up the fame fortnight, I fhall hope
thou wilt meet me with good-hu-
mour.

CON-

CONTENTS.

b 3   *mer's*

CHAP.

b 4 CHAP.

CHAP. XII.

CHAP.

CHAP. XXIII.

CHAP. XXIV.

CHAP. XXV.

CHAP. XXVI.

5 CHAP.

CHAP.

A FORT-

A

FORTNIGHT'S RAMBLE.

CHAP. I.

*A slight Touch of a Margate Hoy ; not to be
read before Breakfast, except you have
been in a Gale of Wind at Sea.*

More than a Life of ERRORS mine hath been,
Yet if I write a *Thought*, the least *obscene*,
May my Young *Oziers* perish—and may I—
Detested live,—and unlamented die.

I WAS sitting very comfortably in Gar-
ner's gallery at Margate, and had forgot
I had taken my passage in the Hoy, until
I saw it warping out. I made the best use
of my legs, took a boat, and was just in
time to be the last to complete a full car-
go of live stock.   We were in hopes of

B   a to-a tolerably good paſſage, but were moſt *rol- lingly* becalmed off the Reculvers. There were many veſſels in ſight, and one man ſaid——" There is ſome comfort in ſee- " ing others in the ſame ſituation with " ourſelves."——" You are a d—d fool " for your pains," ſaid a rough cit; " a calm is a ſtagnation in trade, it can " do no good, but a foul wind to ſome " is a fair wind to others."——" That's " all fair, maſter," ſaid the man at the helm.

It was hot upon deck ; but it was an oven below, and I obſerved moſt of us *amuſed* ourſelves by *complaining* of want of wind, &c. A very quizziſh looking man threw himſelf into a knowing atti- tude, and was apparently making re- marks very earneſtly through the ſpy- glaſs without perceiving the bottom-caſe was on it.—" Pray, Sir," ſays a wag, " is that a ſhip or a brig you are look- " ing at ?"—" The people walk about " ſo, *can't* touch it."—He did not ſeem to enjoy the miftake, but he did not " *touch*" the glafs again during the trip.

After rolling about fome time, whift-ling for a wind as oftlers do to their horfes when drinking, a breeze fprang up, and ficknefs, which had already whitewafhed feveral faces, began to ftir about. I firft obferved it in a young lady, who might have belonged to the family of the " T——'s *," by the flatternly fineries fhe had about her. Her anxious mamma perfuaded her " Deary" to go into the cabin, which was a fignal to be-gin ; and, by what part of curiofity I was induced to follow, I know not.

An old fat man, wedged in a two-armed chair, was confoling and envying her.—" That's *nice*, Mifs—that's brave-" ly done, Mifs !"

I thought I obferved, in the midft of pity and exclamations, he only wanted

* See Goldfmith's Fffays.

in-

inducements to make himfelf fick; and, in confirmation of my furmife, he pulled a bottle of camomile tea out of his pocket, and fwigged heartily.

Mifs went on " bravely." As for the old gentleman, he ftuck clofe to his feat, and COMPLAINED moft bitterly that he could *not* be fick.

We were obliged to drop anchor three times, and performed a voyage in twenty-feven hours which is often done in ten. I lay down for a fhort time in a crib-bed, but was fo befieged by an army of fleas, that I went upon deck, and trudged fulkily the reft of the night.

A Billingfgatean lady chofe to fcold me for walking; but, as I preferred her mellifluent abufe to the ftench of a crowded cabin, and a million of other animals, I was all filence, and roughed it as well as I could. About eleven the next morning a breeze fprang up, which expelled

expelled the clouds both from our faces
and the atmofphere, and a coarfe kind
of wit took place of the fullennefs the
calm had occafioned.

I want words to do juftice to the fatisfaction I felt in going up the river. My
cares vanifhed. I was not only delighted
with the ftreets of fhips we failed through,
but felt an honourable pride in belonging to a country that brings the trade of
all the world into its bofom. I was rich
from feeing the riches round me, and I
thanked my God that I was—a BRITON.

CHAP. II.

A Mail-Coach.

WE fet off in the Leeds mail-coach with a fair wind and a fcowling fky. Our company confifted of my friend, a Sheffield manufacturer, a maiden lady of a certain age with a large band-box, big enough to have purloined a Jemmy Jumps, but which we will fuppofe was better furnifhed with head-ornaments to furprize a country village. We had an opportunity of examining each other's faces for about an hour, and then the evening became very " Sir-ifh, Madam-" ifh," and, on the part of little Shef-field, rather " *fnoring-ifh.*" We wanted a refrefhment of tea to make us chatty. While it was preparing, the honeft
York-

Yorkſhireman took off his wig, and was turning the curls nicely over his fore finger, to the greàt difguſt and furprize of the lady. He tried all that putting on his wig, and begging pardon, could do ; but her ſtomach had received ſo fevere a ſhock, ſhe declared " *the man*" had ſpoilt her breakfaſt. However, ſhe was afterwards pleaſed to open her family budget, and began to be more familiar ; but the poor culprit was never more honoured with a word or even a look. I ſuppoſe a concatenation of ideas would have made her ſick if ſhe had ſeen the wig ; and, he was ſo dumbfounded, we entirely loſt him, until a carriage came to meet her. Her family head bridled up at this diſtinction, and ſhe wiſhed us a " *a good afternoon*" with an air of fuperiority.

Her departure was a ſignal for little Sheffield to begin : his countenance brightened up, and we found him, barring a few grammatical errors, as clever

a man

a man as you could meet with on a fummer's day. He gave us an account of
the trade of his native town, and entered, in a workmanlike manner, into
the manufacturing part of it. He told
us what branches flourish moft now, and
what muft always fucceed; how the
town became commercial, owing to the
pride and feverity of the citizens of York
to fome foreign artifans, by whipping
them out of the city. They not only
thought this ill-judged cruelty meritorious, but keep an holiday in remembrance
of it; and that trade has never held up
its head in York fince, though fo well
fituated for it. In all his conclufions, he
never fpoke favourably of any thing that
had not honefty to regulate it. He had
figned the Addrefs to His Majefty re-
fpecting the proclamation, and faid,
" What could we hope for, more than
" what we have? To be fure, there are
" people that wifh to kick up *bubblety*
" *bubbleties* in Sheffield; but they are
" more NOISE than NUMBERS."

The

The little Wig vaniſhed, and I ef-
ſteemed him full as much as if he had
been decorated with a ramillied peruke.
Had we not been ſo near his houſe, we
ſhould have had a more extenſive leſſon
of ingenuity ; but the misfortune is, man
is too apt to find out the value of any
thing when he is about to loſe it.

It was half paſt two on Monday morning when we reached Leeds, our cloaths
being thoroughly drenched in the boot
of the mail-coach, from the overflowing
of the Trent. The devaſtation in Lei-
ceſterſhire and the adjacent parts of
Northamptonſhire and Nottinghamſhire
was dreadful. The low grounds were
covered with water, and a conſiderable
quantity of hay was hanging on the
hedges in the lanes, and even ſcattered
along the high road. This muſt be very
diſpiriting to the farmers, after a flatter-
ing proſpect of plentiful crops ; but, as
there ought always to be ſome conſola-
tion

tion in every misfortune, let us hope a thick *eddiſh* will leſſen the loſs, and fatten the numerous ſheep with which the banks of the Trent abound. If this river did not ſometimes unſeaſonably overflow, it might be called the Nile of England, from the ſpacious extent of valleys it enriches.

Verſes on the TRENT's being violently flooded July 22, 1792.

Oft does the *Trent*, like Egypt's ſacred *Nile*,
Ruſh o'er its banks, and fertilize the ſoil ;
NURSE OF THE VALES! ſhe fattens as ſhe flows,
And, where ſhe ſpreads, the richeſt herbage grows.
But when the deſolating torrents pour
The branching ſtreams, the farmer's hopes devour,
FIEND OF THE VALES! ſhe ſteals the luckleſs ſheep,
And whirls them in the eddies of the deep.
The new-cut hay, ſo late with pleaſure view'd,
On the wild boſom of the ſtreams is ſtrew'd.
Trees that till now the elements withſtood,
Promiſcuous roll amidſt the frantic flood.
TRIUMPHANT TRENT! indignant in her courſe,
What can withſtand her fury-ſwelling force!
In this the *Rambler*, that ſo tim'rous ran,
Gave drink to cattle, and delight to man !

Clos'd

Clos'd the proud oziers in her amorous fold,
And varied fongs—through various windings told.—
But now, like FRANCE, a vaft confufion reigns,
Fouls her rough courfe, and defolates the plains :
Deftroys thofe flow'rs, her former bounty fed,
And tears the humble from their lowly bed.
Nought is fecure, and friends and foes give way
To the impetuous TYRANTS of the day.

CHAP.

CHAP. III.

*Crofs the Country to Kendal—A Village
Wedding—Fatigue—Covered by Sancho
Panca's incomparable Cloak—The River
Ken—Salmon-leaping—Leven's Park—
The Houfe—A Liquor called Morocco—
Haverfham Village—Sexton, a Man of
Feeling.*

AT five the fame morning we got into
a crofs-country coach for Kendal, paffing along a delightful range of valleys,
frequently keeping the Leeds canal and
a river in view ; on a rifing ground favourable for profpects, we faw a number of people rufh out of a church, and
immediately the bells rang moft merrily.
We defired the coachman to ftop in the
village underneath, until the groupe approached, following a new-married couple ;

ple ; the whole bedizened with ribbands, the bride moft glaringly fo ; large true-blue bows were acrofs the full of her breaft, leffening till they reached the waift, as the poet expreffes himfelf, " fmall by degrees, and beautifully lefs ;" white, red, and every other colour, were confpicuous about her gown and hat, except forfaken green, which, I was glad to obferve, was not worn by one of the throng.——It would have gladdened any heart, to have feen them frifking down the hill ; fuch kiffing, and fuch romping, and fuch laughing, I never heard or faw before. Ruftic happinefs was afloat ; the girls faces were tinged beyond their native bloom, and the maiden's blufh enlivened the lilies around them. The men's legs and arms were as bufy as if they had hung on wires. In an inftant half a dozen youths pulled off their fhoes and ftockings, which gave me an opportunity of noticing their legs had been previoufly girt with party-coloured ribbands. On being ftarted by

the

the bride, they fpanked off as hard as they could, amidft the whoops of the young and old. This I underftand is ˙ a RACE of KISSES, and he who firft reaches the bride's houfe is rewarded with a kifs and a ribband. If they were to have been rewarded with a purfe of gold, they could not have looked more eager; they took different roads, (without heeding the rough ftones they had to encounter) and which, we were told, were previoufly agreed upon, in proportion to the known fwiftnefs of the candidates. We regretted we could not ftay to fee the refult of the Hymenæan race; and left them in the midft of mirth, after a donation which would not take from it, but which was only received on condition of mutually drinking healths, and our accepting a ribband apiece. I got upon the top of the coach, to look at them as long as I could. Marrow-bones and cleavers, thofe fafhionable attendants upon courtly weddings, could not exprefs half the hilarity

which

which we witneffed ; and when the coach fet off, they gave us *breafts-full* of huzzas ; we anfwered them with fuch fincerity, I fhall have a twift in my hat as long as it lafts ; and for fome time after we left them we heard burfts of noife.

I did not obferve the bride was hand-fomer than any of the others, except in her hufband's eyes ; but, if I may judge from what I faw, this healthful valley teems with lufty lads and pretty laffes ; and, if I could have ftayed the day with them, I fhould have found out all their fweethearts.

As long as it was light, variety of fcenes kept us in amufement ; but it was no fooner dark, than the jolting of the clumfy vehicle, flowly dragged along by a lazy pair of horfes, had a moft uncom-fortable effect. I tried to fleep, but tried in vain, and we thought it an age before

before we reached Kendal, which was paft twelve o'clock.

I was no fooner in bed, than fleep, to ufe the language of honeft Sancho Panca, " covered me all over as it were " with a cloak ;" and I could next morning fay with that incomparable proverb-monger, " Heaven's bleffings " reft on that man's head who firft in- " vented it ;" for, it prefented me, after ten hours oblivion, with a cheerful flow of fpirits.   I was prepared for pleafure, my mind as clear as the atmofphere, and at eleven we fet off for Levens along the banks of the Ken, a river which winds its clear courfe amongft rich paf- tures, ftocked with lufty cattle, hang- ing woods, ragged rocks, and thick hay- fields. We were often charmed with the noife of the water foaming down broad weirs. Near one of them, clofe to the powder mills, is a ftout bridge, whofe arches extend from rock to rock, covered with conftant verdure. We fat near it half

half an hour watching abundance of falmon attempting to rife the fall, and
fometimes leaping fideways at a fly, all
of them appearing eager to get up.
Some fucceeded to the firft rife of the
fall, and many fell again into the foam.

How delightfully were we feated, to
hear the mufic of the river !—to fee the
banks cloathed with hanging trees of various green, and under a certain bufhy
part on the oppofite fide large drops
were tinkling down,—oozing through
the projecting roots and mofs, raifing
diftinct and high effects upon the calm
furface underneath !—I felt that charming placidnefs within me, that convinced me I am a fon of Nature. We
left with regret this fcene ; but left it
only to enjoy other beauties.

About a mile from the mills, and to
the left of the river, we entered Leven's
park, paffing through an avenue of lime
and beech trees, ftill keeping the Ken

C   which

which divides the park, well stocked
with deer, on both sides. We had here
a sight of the sands, with two vessels at
anchor. I was struck with the recollection of having seen the sea four hundred
miles off in as many days; but this instantly gave way to the respect I felt, in
admiring the matchless works of Nature.

On approaching the house, we perceived they were busy in housing hay,
and saw a gentleman and two ladies
come out of the garden. Anxious to see
all we could, yet fearful to be thought
intruding, we were asking questions from
one of the hay-makers, when the gentleman politely came to us, and offered
to shew us the house; he was steward to
the lady Andover, and came that day to
overlook the workmen.

The house is turreted, and has stone
winding steps to the leads, from which
you have a prospect charmingly variegated and backed by high mountains.
The rooms are generally of trusty oak,
that

that has hitherto defied Time. Several of them are decorated with the *Bellingham* arms, with a variety of quarterings; these too are painted in the windows. In the great hall there are several coats of armour; and one breaft-plate appears to have had a ball dinted againft it. The Seafons are curioufly expreffed by carved figures in the wainfcot, with verfes under them in old-fafhioned rhyme. The beds are very old, and the curtains are as ragged as a pair of colours that might have belonged to a diftinguifhed regiment that was at the battle of Blenheim. The tapeftry is expreffive of religious and moral fubjects, but does not feem the work of good looms: perhaps it was made before that kind of weaving was brought to the perfection of the laft century *.

---

* In the parlour window *Bellingham* quartering *Burnef-head*; and, on a fcroll, on one fide, *Amicus Amico Ala-nus*; on the other *Belligerus Belligero Bellinghamus*. This couplet was made upon Alan Bellingham, who purchafed Levens, alluding to his focial, and, at the fame time, martial difpofition.

Every

Every part of this refpectable houfe, except what was once wove, may yet laft for ages. The wainfcot and floors are in thorough repair ; and the latter fhone fo bright, I was obliged to tread with caution left I fhould tumble. Much as the Bellinghams have to regret the lofs of thefe eftates, they are in hands that pay attention to repairs, for I never faw an old uninhabited houfe taken fuch care of.

We were regaled by a liquor called *Morocco*, which is made in no other place in the kingdom, and has been peculiar to this houfe time out of mind. It is of a high colour, and is made from malt and hops ; has an acid tafte, and does not ferment ; for, if it was to be left in a glafs for a week, they fay it would be equally good as at the moment it was poured out. I confefs I relifhed it ; *perhaps* becaufe there is none of the fame fort any where elfe.

As

As the steward had business to transact, my friend and I walked to Haversham, a village upon a hill, famous for a school that has produced some great scholars, and recently unfortunate by two youths being drowned near Levens. This accident, which near town would only occasion the general gloom of a minute, seemed to throw sorrow over the face of the sexton, whilst he shewed us the grave; and marked the strong lines of his furrowed countenance with a look of sensibility (I thought), that made an impression in his favour, we have often since spoken of.

The present Bishop of Landaff's father taught this school for many years, with the greatest credit and honour; and at this place that learned and truly respectable Prelate received the first rudiments of his education.

C 3   CHAP.

CHAP. IV.

*A Village Dancing-Mafter—An aged Ma-
tron—Ruftic Politenefs on her Entrance
—A Hornpipe—The Rofe Dance—Farmer's Servant—A Barn Dancing-School
—The Church—Dinner—Return to Levens—The Gardens—Antiquated Houfekeeper—Kitchen-Grate.*

THE fexton was landlord of the Eagle
and Child, and, whilft his good woman
was dreffing our dinner, we were induced,
from feeing a number of boys fhoes, and
hearing the found of a fiddle in a barn,
to become fpectators. About thirty boys
and girls were affembled for a quarter's
inftruction. The mafter had more the
appearance of a man than that of a
dancing-mafter, although he was well
qua-

qualified for the latter in the opinion of the children's parents; I mean no reflection upon the profeſſion, only he did not look like one of thoſe Continental beings, who *cabriol* and *pas-grave* themſelves into the good opinion of faſhion. We will imagine it was a public day, for there were ſeveral ſpectators, and we obſerved an aged matron upwards of eighty, ſupported by two women, bending her ſlow ſteps towards the ſchool. On her entrance there was a general reverence, and one man went into the houſe to bring her a two-armed chair.— If this was not politeneſs, tell me, ye *ſupple* ſons of courts, what it was?

One of the boys danced a hornpipe, with hat aſide and ſtick under his arm, tipping moſt vehemently with heel and toe, but in very good time; the maſter often threw his eyes upon the *ſtrangers*, and I took care to give as much ſatisfaction to my face as I poſſibly could, though really not more than I felt. Af-

C 4   ter

ter the little hero had fweated over his part, nine girls danced a Cotillon in time and ftep that would not have difgraced a ball-room ; and, what had a fingular and ruftic effect, whilft they were going the circle in pairs, the odd number ftepped into the centre, pulled a red rofe from her breaft, which fhe held up as fhe danced round, until fhe led to another ftep, and always, when fhe joined hands with the others, replaced her rofe near cheeks that vied with it in healthful beauty.

Why fhould fo innocent a dance be called a Cotillon ? I think it ought to have an Englifh name.—Where is the harm then in my naming it the ROSE DANCE ?

As there was a tall boy, of about feventeen, that had the appearance of a farmer's fervant, who wanted to dance, my friend was afraid we fhould abafh him if we remained ; fo we

we went away. This lad had the look
of a determined candidate for a prize
dance. He forced out his toes, until he
grinned to it, and looked ſo eagerly at
the dancing girls, I ſhould have thought
they were all his ſweethearts; but, upon
recollection, I am perſuaded he was only
thinking, " if I wur dancing, I'd ne'er
" give out."

As I wiſhed to take in all I poſſibly
could, I obſerved a wooden hoop with
three tin ſockets hanging in the centre
of the barn, to be ready any evening for
a village dance.

From this feat of. ruſtic agility we departed, after ſaying in whiſpers loud
enough to be overheard, " how well
" they danced!" I made my beſt obei-
ſance, and bows and curtſies attended us.
The old good woman put her arms upon the chair, and ſhewed the ſame inclination: I ſat next to her, and beſtowed
ſo many praiſes upon the young ones, I
think

think I gave a gleam of cheerfulnefs to her heart.

I could not help overhearing, whilft one of the boys was dancing his hornpipe, if not in an elegant, in a difficult manner, one of them faid to another, " I con do that." Thefe trifles became fecond nature to me, and I filently gloried in them.

We afterwards went into the church, which is a plain old one; it was burnt down by accident in the year 1601; whereby all the monuments, organ, and other ornaments, were utterly deftroyed, fo that we could only trace the births and burials from the year 1605. In the chancel belonging to the Bellinghams there is a handfome monument upon one of the females, dated 1626, with verfes expreffive of her many virtues, and thofe of her hufband, which has lately been put in repair by a gentleman related to her maiden name, a mark of refpect that deferves to be recorded. On examining the

the regifters, there is no mention of her being buried there.

I hope my reader will pardon me for tranfcribing her epitaph : though it abounds with many quaint expreffions, the fafhion of the times when it was written, it contains many fingular beauties, which I hope will amply atone for its infertion in this work.

" M. S.

Here lyeth the Body of the Lady Dorothie Bellingham, Daughter to Sir Francis Boynton, of Barmfton in the county of York, Knight, and Wife to Sir Henry Bellingham, of Helfington in the County of Weftmoreland, Knight and Baronet. Shee dyed the 23 of January, 1626; ætatis fuæ 32.

> Thrife fixe years told brought up by parents deare,
> Duely by them inftructed in God's feare ;
> Twice feaven years more I lived to one betroth,
> Whofe meanes yea life, were common to us both.
> Seaven children in that fpace to him I browght,
> By nature perfect, and of hopeful growght.
> His parents unto mee deare as myne own,
> Theire loves were fuch as to the world's well known.

But

But ere that one yeare more her courſe had runne,
God in his mercie unto me hath ſhowne,
That all theiſe earthly comforts are but toyes,
Being compared with theſe celeſtial joyes,
Which through the blood of Chriſt are kept in ſtore
For thoſe in whom his word has rul'd before.
To labours borne I bore, and by that forme
I bore to earth, to earth I ſtraight was borne.

In the year 1763, Sir Griffith Boynton, of Burton Agnes in the county of York, baronet, lineally deſcended from the ſaid Sir Francis, repaired and beautified this monument."

By this time dinner was ready; I cannot ſay I ate heartily, my appetite having given way to the ſcenes we had been engaged in. When we aſked what we had to pay, the landlady heſitated, as if ſhe thought ſhe was going to overcharge, and hoped we ſhould " not think eight-pence apiece too much."

In two hours from our leaving Levens we were returned; as Mr. R—— promiſed us the pleaſure of walking with us

to

to Kendal, and fent off his horfe for that purpofe.

The gardens are laid out in the Dutch ftyle, and were planned by king James's gardener, who refided during part of his mafter's troubles with the then owner of it; the perfon who, it is faid, took advantage of the national difturbances of poffeffing the eftate. I have heard that Bellingham followed the fortunes of king James, and, to preferve this eftate in his family, made it over to a man he thought his friend, but who was too partial either to the beauties or the profits of it; and it is even traditioned by poor people of the name of Bellingham, now refiding in Kendal, that the eftate was never paid for.

The gravel walks are broad and long, and each alley and yew tree has its brother. Thefe are too formal to be interefting; befides, they were the heavy tafte of a man that had *deformed* the

beauties

beauties of Nature. The only curiofity I obferved, and which I think is eafily accounted for, is of a tree whofe trunk is cut off a foot from the earth, and whofe branches were engrafted or rather inoculated into another tree ; it was in full foliage, and feemed alive to the bottom of the trunk. Although it may once have been a complete tree, its neighbour becomes the parent, and the fap of it in the Winter muft go into the root.

F After we returned into the houfe, my friend went into the kitchen, and flipt half a crown into the hand of an old curioufly-dreffed houfekeeper, who looked as antiquated as one of the wooden figures in the hall ; fhe *waddled* plenty of dropping curtfies, with a " Thank you, Sir," to every one of them. We had here an opportunity of obferving that the hofpitality of Levens muft have been in the good old Englifh ftyle ; for the kitchen grate is large enough to roaft an

ox,

ox, and I dare fay good eating and morocco were plentifully diftributed.

When the great ALLAN " rul'd this large domain,
" The voice of forrow never mourn'd in vain;
" Sooth'd by his pity—by his bounty fed,
" The rich found comfort, and the aged—bread."
The jovial tenants fill'd the length'ned board,
With ROASTED OX and good *morocco* ftor'd.
But now, though witchcraft in the woods is feen,
And *falmon* ftill enrich the winding KEN,
The name of BELLINGHAM refounds no more,
And HOSPITALITY has left the door.

CHAP.

CHAP. V.

Petrifactions—Kendal Church—A Barber,
a Man of Family.

ABOUT fix we croffed the river, and
paffed through the park amidft thofe
trees that looked fo majeftic when we
were oppofite to them ; two aged beech
trees towered an amazing heighth over
the others, and feemed to have partook
the fame influence of foil, they are fo exactly alike. We continued upon a high
bank until we approached a large piece
that had tumbled into a hole, once famous for drawing falmon, but now their
fafe retreat; this piece is compofed of
petrifactions, a larger quantity than I
ever faw before, and are occafioned from
a lime-ftone fpring.

A per-

A perfon afked permiffion to get fome, and took fo much, that it occafioned an obftruction in future. I mention this, as nothing can be more ill-judged than taking advantage of a wifh to oblige; and by this act, a deep ferpentine part of the river lofes half its beauty, and the beft ftocked part of the fifhery is rendered ufelefs. Thus far the tide comes up, and in fpring-tides the water near the houfe is brackifh.

We fometimes paffed through cornfields, but oftener through pafture, never lofing fight of the river, and we were often entertained by little ftreams tinkling down the hill. I fhould never have been fatigued with this rural walk; but, on entering Kendal, the ftones, which are very fharp and uneven, made my feet fore.

We furveyed the church, which is very large, with handfome ftone pillars.

D

In

In an aile belonging to the Bellinghams,
there is an extraordinary large tomb
without a date, and, from the brafs figure having been purloined, it muft
have fuffered under the depredations of
civil war. There are feveral other monuments of this family ; for there were
at one time a baronet and two knights
of this name in the county, who had feparate houfes, and poffeffed confiderable
property in it.

The hiftory of the County mentions
this family as extinct, yet feveral branches
are ftill in being. The Bellinghams,
of Caftle Bellingham in Ireland, are from
a collateral line ; and Roger Palmer, efq.
of Rufh, and of Palmerftown, in that
kingdom, with his fifter and her children, are immediate defcendants from the
oldeft branch. As it is a family that has
fuffered from civil war, and *other caufes*,
there may be many defcendants who may
have funk into the common mafs of mis-
                              fortunes,

fortunes, and whofe poverty has preserved only the name.

The day following being conftant rain, I have noted down, as well as I could recollect, the pleafures of yefterday, and I truft they will never leave my memory.

There is a barber of the name of Bellingham living under this roof, who fays he is a defcendant ; I underftand, when he gets too much of *Sir John Barleycorn* * in his head, he is wondrous proud of it : his friends fometimes laugh at him, and afk him by what *bye* branch he claims relationfhip. I had fome converfation with him, and he has " *our* family" and " *my* anceftors" very pat.

* A North country expreffion for ale.

CHAP.

CHAP. VI.

Obelisk—Children in Kendal sickly—Indus-
try—New Canal—Tenter-Grounds—A
Man of Ingenuity.

WE went this morning to an obelisk,
erected in 1788 upon a considerable ar-
tificial mount, in remembrance of the
Revolution. I think it is too small an
object both for the subject, and the noble
rise it stands upon ; when we saw it yes-
terday it looked like a tall chimney ; one
would imagine, from its scantiness, there
had been a want of money, but, as it was
built upon so glorious an occasion, it
may rather be attributed to want of
taste. Directly opposite, on the other
side the Ken, stands the remains of the
castle where Catharine Parr was born,
the

the laft wife of Henry VIII. and whofe wife conduct (after fhe had been fecretly impeached), by giving up her religious opinions to thofe of the king, averted her trial, and fhe had the wonderful luck to furvive him. This ruin ftill wears a grand refemblance of what caftles were in former days, though it is mouldering away under the iron hand of Time.

The children in Kendal look very fickly; perhaps they fuffer from the nap of the woollen * manufactory, which is continually flying about, clogging their infant lungs;—but in the neighbourhood, where the air is unadulterated, they are a very rofy race.

There is a meritorious fpirit of induftry amongft them, and the country people, both men and women, were knitting ftockings as they drove their peat-

* Coarfe cloths owe their origin to *Kendal,* where they were firft made in 1390.

carts

carts into the town ; this double way of earning money, not only makes them deferving of the reward, but muft intereft ftrangers in their favour.

Coal is very dear, and they are obliged to ufe peat (a fpecies of turf); but, when the intended canal between Lancafhire and this place is finifhed (which they are afraid will be a tedious time from the number of locks it will require), the cheerful hearth will blaze, and they will have, at a moderate rate, that moft neceffary ingredient in a manufacturing town.

The tenter-grounds on the fides of the little hills refemble the growth of the vine-orchards in Spain ; and, from having much and many coloured cloths upon them, I fhould hope that trade flourifhes. I would wifh to fay fomething in praife of the town, but it is too ill-paved to mind any thing but your feet.

Op-

Oppofite the King's Arms, I thought I obferved an old man I had once known. On feeing him take a pinch of fnuff, I was affured of it; which he was always accuftomed to do, with an air and twift of body peculiar to a man of mental confequence, or as we frequently fee in a perfon that has made the grand tour, and takes this manner of letting you know it.

He was once a capital watchmaker at Minorca, and laft at Gibraltar; and told me with a figh, he was only now a fervant, and that he was obliged to leave the *Old Rock*, becaufe he could not afford to live on it.

After he had recovered himfelf a little, for we were mutually glad to talk of old times, I fell into enquiries about former days, and the look of forrow vanifhed in an inftant. I then afked him after a once extraordinary fine green and

D 4   gold

gold laced coat, I remembered his wearing near five years: when I firſt ſaw it, it was " wondrous, nay paſſing fine ;" it afterwards underwent ſeveral degrees of ſhade, what with the ſun, and time, and ſnuff: and to the laſt made a *famous blockade* appearance.

Imagine to yourſelf—(for I like to bring deſcription as faithful as I can, and I am perſuaded, if this ſhould fall into the hands of any of my old brother-ſoldiers, they will eaſily recognize poor ABRAHAMS)—imagine then a middle-ſized man, with a rubicund face, and hair *bien frizzled*; toes turned out, particularly one foot, from the leg having been three times broke ;—do not forget his green and gold, and, I have to add, a cock and pinched hat equally ruſty, with a break in the centre, from the polite bows he always made, and with a pair of brownified ſilk ſtockings—ſuch was once poor Abrahams. Now he has ſhort hair, a plain coat, and worſted ſtock-

ſtockings. The only daſh of finery, was a coarſe ſpotted velvet waiſtcoat; but whoever ſees him would ſay, " that man " has known better days."

I was ſorry to ſee him ſo reduced. He was always reckoned clever in buſineſs, and would moſt willingly have given a deſcription of the inſide of a watch, without expreſſing the leaſt diſpleaſure at the ignorant or inquiſitive. I have idled away many an hour in his ſhop, and would not forget him in his poverty. He acknowledges his imprudences, and ſays he ſhall never leave off his cuſtom of " *ſwigging* away a few days.".

He tells a ſtory of his father being ſo complete a workman, that he once made a chain of ſteel ſo very fine, he had faſt-ened a flea by the leg with it. This ſtory has been offered to Baron Munchauſen, for his next edition; but I can inform the good folks of Kendal, there are many people who have ſeen ſuch a thing.
When

When he firſt ſpoke of it, a man left the
company, and brought in a whetſtone,
and laid it before him. Abrahams had
not been long enough amongſt them to
know the meaning of it, and thought it
was for him to ſwear by. He took it up,
kiſſed it, and ſwore it was true. This
has occaſioned a ſtanding jeſt againſt
him, and I think in the end will drive
him out of the town.

I introduce this to reſcue him from
laughter. Nothing can be more uncom-
fortable than being the butt of a country town. The ignorant may laugh at
his follies, but it would be more to their
credit if they could imitate his ingenuity.

When I arrived at the King's Arms
the other evening, I was ſo diſpleaſed
with my fatigue I thought it a bad inn:

* It is a cuſtom in the North, when a man tells the
greateſt lye in company, to reward him with a whetſtone, which is called " Lying for a whetſtone."

two

two days have convinced me that Mrs. Mafterfon is civil and intelligent, and you have every thing in peace and plenty. The houfe is a large old ftragling one. There are two galleries leading to the bed-rooms; and I would advife you to make a crofs, to know which to go by.

CHAP.

CHAP. VII.

*Ing's Chapel—Induſtry rewarded—Benevo-
lence—A firſt Sight of the Lakes—Boats
upon Windermere—Amblefide.*

ABOUT ſix miles from Kendal, we
ſtopped to ſee Ing's chapel, rebuilt by a
Mr. Bateman, who was born in this pa-
riſh, of poor parentage. He went through
a progreſſive ſucceſs of induſtry, and was
entruſted by his maſters in London to
tranſact their buſineſs at Leghorn. Fortune befriended him, and he amaſſed
immenſe riches. He had ſo juſt a regard
for his native place, he remitted money
to repair the chapel, and at the ſame
time ſent moſt beautiful marble to inlay
the flooring, which is elegantly finiſhed,
the ſteps only leading to the altar being
of

of ſtone. The ſeats are uniform, and of a commodious ſize.

He not only gave this tribute to the church, but left alſo one thouſand pounds to the poor *. He lived not to re-return home, and his executors had the finiſhing of it, which is expreſſed on a ſtone affixed to the ſteeple.

It is ſaid the little of his property remitted to England was all that was ſaved to his family, and, whether by loſſes or extravagance the remainder was diſperſed, report diſagrees. I cannot, from what I heard, ſpeak with confidence upon the ſubject ; I only wiſh to

* It ſeems a matter of doubt, whether the liberality of this worthy man will be attended with thoſe good effects he piouſly intended, as his beneficence draws numerous poor into the townſhip, who endeavour to gain ſettlements, in order to partake of his donation. Hence perpetual ſquabbles and law-ſuits—ſo that the beſt intentions are but too often rendered ineffectual, or of little conſequence, by the perverſeneſs or avarice of mankind.

do

do honour to the well-beftowed munifi-
cence of this grateful man, and fay to
the rich, moft humbly quoting the language of our Saviour, Go thou and
do likewise.

I had not retained Mr. Bateman and his
chapel long in my mind, before we faw
a filver line ftealing down a fteep mountain right ahead of us : we fuppofed it
occafioned by yefterday's rain, and while
I was ftraining my eyes to look at it to
the left, we caught a firft fight of Windermere. Here I could not help dwel-
ling, or rather I wifhed to dwell, for I
called to the poftillion not to go on fo
faft, without perceiving we were defcending a fteep hill. We again loft the
lake ; but the next rifing prefented us
the rivulet and Windermere, and I did
not omit paying a vifual attention to the
little ftranger, which I knew in one minute I was to lofe. Her extenfive Neighbour was boldly to the left of us, and,
exclufive of the iflands, and moun-

tains, and woody borders, half a dozen boats were failing under a frefh wefterly breeze.

As you enter Amblefide, there are fome of the loftieft pines I ever faw, taller, I dare fay, than any to the fouth-ward of them. Though the pine is a melancholy tree, it is here feen amongft fuch cheerful verdure, it is worth ad-miring as a contrafting fhade, and, to thofe who have never vifited Northern countries, for the height it grows; and when we confider the quicknefs of their growth, and the fhelter they yield to the youthful oak and other ufeful plants, the obferver will of courfe have a tributary thought in its favour.

CHAP.

CHAP. VIII.

A kind of Apology for myself—Rydal Water-falls—Rydal Lake—Amphitheatre around it—Grafsmere—A Country Ale Houfe—Went upon the Lake—An Attempt at Defcription—A Prayer for the Inhabitants—Crooked Chimney an Eye-fore.

AFTER a dinner of moft excellent trout, we commenced our ramble.

I take an opportunity of mentioning, the perfon out of friendfhip for whom I take this journey is the fole director of it. I follow no written guide, left I fhould enter too fully into other people's ideas, and not give a native fcope to my own. I fhall do the beft I can, frequently writing upon the fpot whence

3   the

the object ſtrikes me, which may occaſion both the *preſent* and *preter-perfect tenſes* in the ſame chapters. I do not know how to avoid incommoding my readers with tautology, but hope they will follow me with more good-nature than criticiſm ; yet, I have that attachment for truth, I would rather feel the critic's *laſh*, than intentionally miſrepreſent.

Our firſt walk was to Rydal Hall. The youngeſt daughter of the head huſbandman waited at a gate to attend company to the caſcades ; ſhe led us through the woods up a ſteep cauſeway to the higheſt water-fall, which ſurprizes by a ſhort turn to the left, ruſhes about forty-five yards into a declivity, and then roars down the hill. The mouth may be about two yards and a half wide.

We deſcended a hundred yards, and then came ſuddenly upon another, which did not fall ſo ſteep, but was ſo overcharged with water, it occaſioned a thin

E   ſheet

sheet to spread over an adjoining rock, separated by a sharp point, and seemed, from the prismatic effect on the spray, to act like a reflecting rainbow to a larger one.   After satisfying the eye, we declined lower than the house, along winding slate walks, plentifully supplied with bilberries, and edged with ever-greens, well intersperfed with the care-less labernum ; this road leads us to an old wainscoted room darkened by sur-rounding shades, which presented a cas-cade arched by trees, and back-grounded by an ancient bridge, with the verdure seen under it.   At the instant I am wri-ting, a man with his heyday drefs, with a rake and a stone bottle, is passing over the bridge : the back shade makes his frame and drefs so distinct, I shall never forget the figure..   It would have been a happy moment for a painter.

We afterwards pursued the Keswick road along the banks of Rydal lake ; the beautifully mis-shapen mountains around

us

us formed a grand amphitheatre. Some
of them were fortified by the Romans;
and feem deferving of them, in their Au-
guftan grandeur.

We afcended the weftern hill, and had
by degrees a complete view of the com-
pact—THE RURAL GRASSMERE.—We directed our courfe towards the church at
the top of the lake, where we were told a
man of the name of Robert Newton kept
a public-houfe, and that he was an intelligent man. On feeing near the church
a fign-poft, we concluded it to be the
place. We were amufing ourfelves with
the neat rufticity around us, when the
landlady came in, and faid her hufband
was amongft his hay; but, obferving him
refting upon a ftyle, very likely induced
to linger about to know if he was wanted, fhe called to him,—" *Robert, tha mun*
" cum in." Newton is fince removed
into a new houfe, which I hope is well
accuftomed.—I recommend to his good
woman to make plenty of preferved

goofe-

goofeberries—which, I am certain, will be as well relifhed as "Mrs. Primrofe's "goofeberry wine"—and *then*, travellers, tafte it with fome of her rich creams; and there can be no doubt but it will pleafe the palate, (no difparagement to Mrs. Primrofe, as much as her wine could do). —Do not be fearful of want of room: befides this new houfe, he has built a barn, fo capacious, my friend in a heavy fhower rode into it, and hardly ftooped.

After fome expreffions of civility, he told us, he was going to take up his floats in Graffmere, and fhewed us a pike of four pounds he had caught in the morning. This was an opportunity we could not omit, and we propofed going with him.

But, I muft firft tell you, this public-houfe was not diftinguifhed by prints expreffing rules for drinking,' but by "King Charles's good rules;"—a picture of the purfuit under the royal oak, and

and a large one explaining the twelve months, with inftructive verfes under each of them. Behind his cottage he had dammed in a fmall ftream, which ferved as a receptacle for trout, pike, and perch, to be ready whenever he wanted them ; and he had the precaution to flant fome large flag ftones, for the fifh to retire under in hot weather.

An old man upwards of eighty affifted in rowing ; and upon our not immediately finding fome of the floats, where he had expected them, he faid, " I'me keeping a *fhairp* eye after them." We did not take any fifh, and Robert feemed more difappointed on our account than on his own.

Thefe floats are fhaped like bar-fhot, or, what may be more generally underftood, like dumb bells. The line is rolled round the bar, and although it may be entangled amidft the weeds, there is no danger of lofing it, even if they

E 3   leave

leave them out all night; for, theft is a phænomenon in this valley. But I was so much engaged with all around me, I did not care about fish.

Whilst rowing slowly on, we rested upon our OARS to attend to the effect of cannon, which, we afterwards learnt, were fired at Belle-isle Island on Windermere—in compliment to the *Marquis of Lansdown*, who was upon a visit to Mr. *Curwen*. It is impossible to conceive a more delightful retreat for a *busy statesman* to retire to—in order to relieve the mind from the effect of past fatigue, and to enable it to bear future *trouble*.

Grassmere is named from a green rump-shaped island, on which there are many sheep, an outhouse for shelter, and occasionally a couple of cows : this verdant spot is four acres and a half in circumference, with a low shelter of trees to the south-west.

The

The diftance between Seat Sandal* and the oppofite mountain † exhibits a grand canopy; and in the valley, or, as it is here called, the GRAIN, the road to Kefwick runs. Thefe mountains are fo much alike, it may not be improper to call the one *brother*, and the other *fifter*; as, in the proportion of my mind, they are fimilar to the difference in fize between male and female. This fpace is rendered more folemn by dark clouds tumbling into the valley; yet the fun piercing over them fhews a diftant Alp tinged with watery beauty.

On approaching the eaftern entrance we obferve two farm houfes, which during three winter months never experience the cheering rays of the fun. The fteeple, and what I can fee of the church, embofomed in trees, are delightfully pic-

* From its fandy front.
† Steel Fell.

turefque.

turefque.—May the God of Heaven
blefs the inhabitants that perform their
prayers on its rough oak benches !

To the right they have been cutting
down fome valuable underwood, which
rather hurts the look of the *tout enfemble :*
but certainly the hufbandman ought to
reap the fruits of his labour.

Scotch cattle are feeding amidft the
woods, and fheep are beautifully dotted
upon the hill, at the foot of which we
are going to land. This is common
land, and fo different from the others,
there is not an inclofing wall, or a tree
to be feen. Our guide left us, and it
was with diffidence he accepted a trifle.

We have agreed to dine at his houfe
on Sunday, and he is afterwards to go
with us to the fummit of Helm Crag, a
fteep hill, that apparent lyover-hangs the
Kefwick road.

Graff.

Graſſmere is a handſome ſloping brook to Rydal, and in the ſeparation becomes the Rathay. We occaſionally ſtopped on the ſoft land on its margin, and took a view of the whole. I will endeavour to give a deſcription.

The formidable heavens to the Weſt ſet off the wild grandeur of the mountains, and over our head they are as ſerene as the valley they adorn; to the North a large table hill, with a thick miſt daſhing over it; the South is diſtinguiſhed by a golden appearance from the ſun's tinging the clouds, and ſhews ſome ſtraggling trees ſo diſtinctly, we can delineate the ſeparation of leaves.

If ſights like theſe cannot fill the mind with reverence, it muſt be undeſerving of enjoying them!

We returned by a good foot-path, and were glad to find the landlord had
changed

changed our room for one that had a different afpect. There is a crooked chimney right before the other, which fo obftructs the fight of Windermere, as to take away the pleafure of it.

Since the firft edition of this Ramble, I underftand, the crooked eye-fore is taken down.

CHAP.

CHAP. IX.

WINDERMERE.

Too much Description—Thompson's Island.

AT the head of this QUEEN of the Lakes* are some neat houses that cannot be exceeded for freshness of air and sweetness of prospect. We were apprehensive of the day, as we were attended to the Lancashire side of the lake with a mizzling rain; but, if you please, you may mark the progress.

The sun pierces upon the Rydal mountains that back-ground the head of the lake, shewing them in just light and

* Windermere is the largest of the lakes.

shade.

ſhade.—Rydal Hall appears about the centre, commanding a moſt delightful view, and in return is equally worthy of notice. When I ſaw it yeſterday, the modernizing alteration took from the pleaſure I ſhould have had, could I have ſeen it in its antient form ; but the diſtance we are now from it takes away the objection.

Langdale Pikes hold up their ragged heads in ſhapeleſs horror, as if they had been thrown out by a moſt violent convulſion of nature.

Low Wood is thickly wooded, and ſhews the ſnug roof of a farm-houſe about one-third of the way up it; at the foot is Low-Wood Inn, a neat object, with about fifty ſcattered fields near it.

Calf Parrick Crag is oppoſite the inn, and we are cloſe rounding into its bay: this point takes away many old views, and opens upon new ones.

About

About two miles to the left is Brad
Rifen, a large field full of fheep, and
furrounded by wood; about a mile farther a light-green field, fhaped like a
tumulus, fkirts the view.

The rain has ceafed, columns are flying about, and the fun has dried the paper upon which my pencil is faithfully
writing.

We open the little village of Bownefs,
and a fquadron of feven cutters prefent
themfelves with pendants and colours flying, failing under different tacks: the
farm-houfe I before remarked is called
Dove Neft, and is become a well-placed
object. The fields in front have a regular flope, and are ornamented with
the exhilarating fight of the farmers
fpreading out their hay, which gives us
hopes we fhall have a fine day, as they
know more of this climate than we do.

From

From High-ray Bay Langdale Pikes appear over a wooded hill : we have like-wife the Old Man and Wedderlamb, which become interefting, though they are barren ; for, the *leffer* hills, which compofe the fore part, are of variegated verdure. At the weftern extremity of Wedderlamb it is raining as hard as it can pour, and on the adjacent hills the fun and clouds are playing fantaftically.

We are opening Colgarth—but I am taken off by one of the Pikes, which, as the boat rows flowly on, refembles a Cardinal's cap, fhewing itfelf above the centre of a very green hill.

The fquadron is manœuvring with feeming nautical fkill, having no lee fhore to be afraid of, which was fo great a *bugbear* this day fourteen years *.— Colours are hoifted upon Belle Grange Point, to inform the people the mafter is

* 27th July.

on

on the ifland. This deep part of the lake is famous for char, which are ufu-ally taken between November and April. Though covered from the breeze, we are often refrefhed with the fragrance of new-mown hay. The boats are near Dove Farm, and feem appendages to the meadows : much as I have been ac-cuftomed to the fea, I cannot fay I ever faw a prettier water-fight before. We went on fhore at the Flag-Staff, and had a full command of Belle-Ifle, an ifland formed about the middle of the lake, nearly two miles in circumference. We fee Bownefs church, and a chain of low hills partly covered with heath, appa-rently extending to the extremity of the lake, and occafionally interfperfed with fmall fields and fome wood.

I do not doubt but Colgarth is large and comfortable within, but at this dif-tance I think the windows have a pigeon-hole look. About one, we landed upon Thompfon's Ifland, from which we have

a fair

a fair fight of Belle-ifle houfe and plea-
fure-grounds, appearing to be laid out
in much modern tafte. This ifland is
near two others, called *Lilies of the Valley*, which are deferving of their name ;
for, they are beautiful little fpots.

After a plentiful meal near fome wild
myrtle, and amidft afh and other trees, I
penetrated through the wood, and am
feated unfeen, to admire Rydal Head
and the courfe we have taken. The
wind has driven the clouds before the
fun, and left an azure over the lake
which has changed the dun colour of
it to a reflected blue, and makes the
whole placidly new. The flag-ftaff divides the vale of Rydal, and I have the
fquadron on a returning tack rounding
the point. Colgarth is a pleafant white
object, without any other Houfe to be
feen.——A fweeping mountain over Troutbeck * Dale forms a fullen crefcent with

* So called from the quantity of trout the brook fupplies.

a camel's

a camel's protuberance on its back, and
which makes one of thofe deformed reflections upon another mountain, that
we may call difguftful, though but a
fhadow. A mufket is juft fired near
fome reverberating hills;—nor muft I
pafs unnoticed the bleating of fheep on
the Lower Fells, the ruftling of the
wind, and the poppling of the lake;
thefe founds are diftinctly heard, and
undifturbed by difcordance, and join
with *fight* in filling up the pleafures of
the mind.

When I had taken a *fill*, I returned to
my friend on the dinner fide of the
ifland; the view is confined, and Belle-
ifle territory is a ftudied pleafure-ground,
with many fheep upon it grazing to a
bounding fhrubbery.

Houfes in fituations like thefe become
fecondary objects, and can only be noted
as fpots in the wild grandeur around
them, and in proportion to the benevo-

F   lence

lence of the owner—a virtue not wanting here.

Sewry Heights have a cool look, and muſt be very valuable every fourteen years, when the wood is cut down for charcoal.

We proceeded to a point where there is a ferry to convey carriages that paſs between Hawkeſhead and Kendal : after walking up a ſmall hill, we ſaw the outlet of Windermere, then croſſed to the oppoſite ferry in front of Belle-iſle, and ſaw eight cutters and a yacht at anchor.

The houſe is ſhaped like a low watchtower, ſeemingly built to catch every object about the lake. The portico gives it a handſome front ; but I want taſte to admire any other part of it ; and even the pillars, when we had a ſide view in the ſhade of the evening, ſeemed as if

4   they

they were *walking* away with the houſe to Bow-neſs. I obliged Robin Partridge, *contrary* to his wiſhes, to acknowledge the reſemblance.

CHAP.

CHAP. X.

WINDERMERE.

Bow-nefs—An Adder—Robin Partridge's Finger, and an old Irifhwoman's Charms —Robin angry becaufe I want Faith— Remnants of Furnefs Abbey Window— To fee Windermere to Advantage.

AFTER landing at Bow-nefs, we went into a fummer-houfe, at the end of a diminutive bowling-green; and I will now mention an inftance which happened at the oppofite ferry, that fhews the fuperftition of the country people.

I faw an adder in a wall : the guide's fore-finger was laft year bitten by one, and it muft have been a very venomous hurt.   He faid—" I fhould have loft my
" loife

" loife if I'd naw found an Irifhmon to
" lay houd of it and ftrouk it, and du-
" ring th' time he did it, I fealt no pean."
—I afked him, if he did not think if an
Englifhman had rubbed it, it would have
done equally well, or if he was not obliged to his good habit of body for the
cure.—" Not I—an Englifhmon cu'd
" naw chearm away th' fting"—and, by
way of elucidation, told a ftory of " a
" Feact," that he faw happen when a
boy.

" An old Irifhwoman mead a ring
" round an adder, and it cu'd naw geet
" out of it ; hua then repeated fome GI-
" BERISH, weet her finger wi her fpittle,
" ftroaked it crofs its back, and it deed."

I fhould have laughed moft heartily
at honeft Robin Partridge, if I had not
been convinced he fpoke from fimplicity
of mind ; and I think I did rather fink
in his good graces by not having any
faith in the Hibernian touch.—May not

this

this man be a relation to the once famous Almanack-maker?

I went up a fmall hill near the inn, whence I had a view of the whole of the lake: an indefcribable fcene was open to me, and I enjoyed it for half an hour.

Reader! haft thou not, when ftretched along a verdant eminence, planted thy head upon thine arm,—and taken full fcope of the extenfive views;—fo was I in mental banquet, when my friend, who had left me at the ferry, returned at feven o'clock, and recovered me from the reverie.—My wrift, which had fo long fupported a heavy head, twinged moft painfully; and which I had not felt until *awoke* from admiring the variegated beauties, the bountiful hand of Nature had lavifhed around.

The rector, who accompanied my friend, was fo obliging as to fhew us his church; I never faw a neater one; and, though

though it is not adorned with a marble flooring, it is in every other respect equal to Ing's chapel, and confiderably fuperior in fize.

It is interesting from writing, in an-tient characters, which decorates the walls with wholefome verfes from the Bible, dated 1629, but more fo by a rich painted window full of fcriptural and hiftorical allufions, with patchings of armorials of fome of the county gentry: thefe are too much in piecemeal to be fully explained, but they muft be a no-ble treat to the experienced Antiquary.

Our Saviour upon the crofs, with blood flowing from the wounds, with the difciples and female attendants around him, are luckily the moft central and perfect figures, and, as we had not long to ftay, took up moft of our thoughts. I obferved St. George and the Dragon; and in the left corner a fmall figure at prayers, with a mantled cloak and the

F 4   bonnet

bonnet of one of our kings. Towards the top, which feparates the fcriptural from the armorial expreffions, is a round pane with the arms of England and France encircled by the Garter—" HONI SOIT " QUI MAL Y PENSE."—I think the little figure is meant for Edward the Third, the inftitutor of that order, and the pofture a humiliating acknowledgement for the many victories he gained ; and, it is well known, that monarch, with all his foibles, had a fenfe of Religion. We may, with probability, imagine it the work of that reign * ?

In

* " The window confifts of feven compartments, or partitions. In the third, fourth, and fifth, are depicted, in full proportion, the Crucifixion, with the Virgin Mary on the right, and the beloved Difciples on the right fide of the crofs ; angels are expreffed, receiving the facred blood from the five precious wounds. Below the crofs are a groupe of monks in their proper habits, with the abbot in a veftment ; their names are written on labels iffuing from their mouths ; the abbot's name is defaced, which would have given a date to the whole. In the fecond partition are the figures of St. George and the Dragon. In the fixth is reprefented St.
Ca-

In the demolition of the abbey of Furnefs, when the barbarous order of a ra-
pacious king took away the emoluments
of the abbeys, regardlefs of the ornaments, this WRECK of the great window
was buried, and, at a more enlightened
period, it was dug up and placed in its
prefent ftation.

Neither my time nor my ftudies allow
me to write with *information* of this cele-

Catharine, with the figures of mitred abbots, and underneath them two monks dreffed in veftments. In the
middle compartment above, are finely painted, quarterly,
the arms of England and France, bound with the garter,
and its motto, probably done in the reign of Henry the
Third. The reft of the window is filled up by pieces of
tracery, with fome coats armorial, and the arms of feveral benefactors ; amongft whom are Lancafter, Urf-
wick, Harrington, Kirkby, Prefton, Middleton, and
Millam. The Flemings paternal coat (viz. Gules, a fret
of fix pieces Argent) is in divers parts of this window,
fome of them with a file of five points, or lambeaux,
which began to be ufed about the reign of King Edward
the Firft, as a difference for the eldeft fon, the father
being living." Burne's Hiftory of Weftmoreland.
This window was purchafed by the parifhioners of
Windermere, from Furnefs Abbey.

3 brated

brated relick, but I hope my memory
has been faithful in recollecting what I
faw.

There is a curious epitaph, dated
1627, on an old gentleman, written by
himfelf.

After this feaft of Reafon and Religion, between eight and nine we reimbarked for our return: the great ifland
and leffer ones, which are trimmed cir-
cularly, look well, and the fight is much
improved from the fquadrons having
their colours ftill flying, though the
commanding officer deferves a reprimand
for not ordering them to be *doufed* at fun-
fet—A NAUTICAL HINT.

We had a fmall rain for half a mile,
but the heavens were grand, and promifed favourably; the moon fhone on
the fcarce curling water, and the views
were foftened by her beams. We rowed
flowly on, and as we paffed between Low
Wood

Wood and the beach, where we em-
barked, feveral guns were fired; the echo
was oppofite, and then ran along Rydal
hills. The water became glaffy, and as
we got in with the head of the bay, the
echo varied with additional flaps, and
trembled more in departure: it was half
paft nine when we landed, and the
great chafm to the Weft ftill marked
the influence of the fun.

To fee Windermere to advantage, you
ought to begin at the extremity, and you
will find every profpect improve until
you open the Rydal mountains.

CHAP.

CHAP. XI.

PATTERDALE.

Large Farms detrimental—A Walk to Patterdale—More Defcription—Six magnificent Mountains—The Vale of Patterdale—Wild Strawberries—The Church-Yard—The King of Patterdale's Palace—Could not get Admittance—The Prince's Sons fine Children—Lyulph's Tower—March, quick one—Receipt againft Fatigue—A hearty Meal—The Landlord—A Coin found—Cuftom relative to ftraggled Sheep—A Maid of Honour—The QUEEN THIRSTY.

WE fet out at nine along a good chaife road, feeing on the hill, to the right, a large fpace of ground, well drained, and all of it beautifully laid out: it is the

pro-

property of a perfon who is very charitable to the poor, but the farmer fays
he has too much in hand : I have heard
feveral of them fay they neither *think* he
will meet with fuccefs, nor *wifh* that he
may.

I never think it a pleafant fight to fee
a rich man keep more land in his poffeffion than what adds to his domeftic
amufements : many farms fcatter cheerfulnefs amongft the occupiers, and plenty
amongft the people ; and we could not
help obferving with concern, it is too
much a cuftom to monopolize land ; the
poor complain of it, though not with
loudnefs, yet with SORROW.

We laboured up a hill about three
miles, and at every reft took a retrofpec-
tive view of the valley, a fheet of Windermere, a *tarn* behind it, and Hawkfhead.
We then dropt down Kirkftone, at the
commencement of the parifh of Patterdale : at the bottom of the road, part

of

of Bridder Water looks as if *embayed* in mountains, with trees and copfe-wood on its margin, giving it the appearance of a fifh-pond in a large garden; winding on we come to a fmall waterfall, of above one hundred yards defcent, widening at the bottom, and which is rendered ftill more beautiful by my friend's removing fome obftructing ftones; it then joins a little ftream, and finks under the road. Lower down we opened upon another hill, and perceived another cafcade; we have now three in fight, and, although the *leaft*, that which I firft noticed is the favourite.

On entering the vale of Hartfop, we have a full command of Bridder-water. This fmall dale, though not cloathed with good grafs, is prettily wooded, and is beneath a femicircular mountain with mifhapen interftices, forked like lightning, but which are the effects and conveyers of torrents; this rugged mountain hangs *proudly* over the valley, as if

to

to deter any inhabitants from fixing there, and I obferved but one houfe.

A heavy fhower detained us under a rough wall, which has luckily fome ftones taken out, and gives me an opportunity of keeping my paper dry. We then proceeded along Bridder-water, occafionally feeing the filver-tailed wheat-ear, fearfully endeavouring to hide itfelf from the fhadow of a cloud, and likewife feveral broods of wild ducks.

Croffing the old bridge at the foot of the *tarn*, we command a grand view of *Six Grains*, which are valleys feparated by immenfe mountains. Dods is the fulleft promontory I ever faw, and feems as if it had bulged out from, and overgrown, a crefcent-formed hill ; nor muft I pafs unnoticed a mountain with a folitary tree near the fummit, which is covered from the North-weft wind by a bending rock.

The

The varieties of verdure, heath, **and** barrennefs, upon thefe tremendous mountains, according to the influence of the fun, and the roughnefs intermixed, give a folemn force to the mind, yet makes it pleafed to enter THE VALE OF PATTER-DALE.

We pafs along this extenfive dale, with a river running through meadows, in the midft of harveft: to the right, hanging woods, and we fee a very irregular cafcade fhowering down the hill, which we carry in fight near a mile, frequently feeing it through trees: to the left, the wood was too thick and clofe to defcribe, but was equally welcome, by prefenting us with plenty of wild ftrawberries of that pleafant acid fo refrefhing to the thirfty. We paffed feveral wretched cottages, and came fuddenly to the King's Arms, with a firft fight of Ullfwater. After ordering dinner

TO THE LAKES. 81

ner we followed the road to the church *,
which *has* the only burial ground I ever
faw without a grave-stone.

The quiet inhabitants of this kingdom
are content to reft with their forefathers,
having one green clod to cover them all,
which may be in perfection when tombs
fhall be no more.—I could not have felt

* " When at Patterdale I had heard of the following
inftance of frugality in a former curate, but I was fo
much taken up with living characters I could not fufficiently truft my memory to relate it. On reading an old
Gentleman's Magazine I abftract the following :

" January 31, 1766, died the Reverend Mr. Mattinfon,
" curate of Patterdale, in Weftmoreland, for 60 years.
" The firft infant he chriftened after he got Holy Orders,
" when fhe was nineteen years old agreed to marry him ;
" and he afked her and himfelf in the church. By his
" wife he had one fon and three daughters, and married
" them all in his own church himfelf. His ftipend,
" till within thefe twenty years, was only £.12. *per*
" *annum*, and never reached to £.20. yet of this, by the
" help of a good wife, he brought up his four children
" very well, and died at the age of 83, grandfather to
" 17 children, and worth ONE THOUSAND POUNDS."

G   more

more reverence (perhaps not fo much) had I trod amidft "the ftoried urns or "animated bufts," or had I feen the moft fuperb maufoleum that was ever raifed at the Shrine of Pride.—No !—nothing was ever formed by the hand of man that could equal this verdant monument.

On looking through the windows, I could diftinguifh no ornaments to defcribe. It appeared the pooreft church I ever faw ; but it is the houfe of God, and it is exceeding our duty to find fault with it. The rotten trunk of a yew tree of amazing circumference, with *embers* of life ftill left, may challenge in age any one in Great Britain, as I am told it once did in fpreading branches. From this unlettered laft retreat of villagers, we had not far to go to the palace ; a palace that muft ever be remembered for being the refidence of the KING OF PATTERDALE ; and, from what we had heard of his Majefty, it was impoffible

3   poffible

poffible not to have the greateft wifh to
fee him. Curiofity, that fpur to idle
minds, got the better of politenefs; and
we went up a large flight of broken fteps,
and knocked at an old houfe that had
once been handfome, and would ftill be
fo in a picture. After a perfevering
knock of fome minutes, a female fervant
came to us, and we made an excufe by
enquiring after profpects; but vain was
our hopes of feeing, for the prefent, the
Royal Family. Two fine healthful-look-
ing grand-children came out; my friend
gave each of them a Druidical half-penny *, the fight of which, and the ancient look of the palace, made me think
I had fallen fome centuries back; but, as
an audience was at this time impractica-
ble, I muft quit their majefties for the
prefent; "*but more of them hereafter.*"

We went along the lake rifing by a
good road, moft of the way covered by

* Coined by the Paris Mine Company.

trees,

trees, with only a partial fight of the water, until we came to an opening which gave us two miles of the lake, and three barren iflands; on one of them the country people have heaped in rough ftones the figure of a man; it being cuftomary for every perfon to add a ftone to different fhaped heaps in places feldom frequented.

The whole was bounded by Lyulph's Tower* in Gowborough Park, built lately by the Duke of Norfolk, in memory of a Saxon hero, and as a fporting retreat. This caftle, fo near its majeftic neighbours, has an effect that fuits the tafte

---

* Probability why it is called Lyulph's tower. Edmund the Firft, who cleared his country of robbers, and conquered Cumberland, was affaffinated at a Feaft by a daring outlaw of the name of Leolf, and who, probably, was one of his Cumberland enemies;—and as thefe parts were much covered with wood, they might be retreats for robbers, who were not held in deteftation in the reign before Edmund I. · He was the firft monarch that made it death to fteal, and then only the oldeft man in the gang was executed.

of

of the fcene, and fhews the juft one of
the noble owner. We proceeded to the
end of Patterdale, which feparates Weftmoreland from Cumberland. On a rock
lately defpoiled of its trees, we had a
moft extenfive view, rounding an elbow
of rich land, and prefenting at a diftance
Stainmore hills, and part of Yorkfhire:
the mounts behind us were thick cloathed, and there is an almoft perpendicular one (conical topped) crowned with
trees.

We were no fooner in the road, but
we recollected five hours walking required a hearty meal, and we trudged
merrily back again to a quick march—I
always whiftle when I find myfelf growing fatigued. The inftant we arrived
we fell-to. What we had for dinner
was of no confequence, never troubling
ourfelves about fuch trifles; for, we were
determined to be pleafed with whatever
was laid before us.

G 3   The

The landlord had been in his hay-field. We afked him to fit down, and we found him a well-informed man; every one in this part of the world learns to read and write; and, although they work hard, they take care their children are properly inſtructed. He is a very clever fellow, and had penciled upon the wall the view from his houſe; he had ſome choice books in the room where we dined, and he converſed ſo *ſenſibly*, I felt even refpeÆt for him; and a man muſt have degraded himſelf to have imagined he was his ſuperior.

In ſpeaking of coins, he ſhewed us a ſilver one of the 3d of Elizabeth, which he dug out of his orchard two years ago; I never ſaw one in higher preſervation, and, what I am pleaſed to add, I purchaſed it for half a crown, which I intend keeping in remembrance of the Vale of Patterdale. The landlord's mother,

ther, who is feventy-five years of age, never recollects a piece of money being found in the valley before.

When sheep stray in thefe counties it is not ufual for the owners to look after them.

There is an agreement between Patterdale, Matterdale, and Legerthwaite, that is too great a credit to the inhabitants to omit fpeaking of, as it marks a liberal-minded people.

They meet on St. Martin's day, to exchange their strayed sheep; every farmer bringing thofe which do not belong to him; no other expence is thought of, but the general one incurred, by feasting on roaft geefe and ale; and they are fo happy with each other, they fometimes make a fecond day.——I would walk a hundred miles to be prefent at fuch a fight.

G 4
Whilft

Whilſt we were talking, we ſaw an ambling old woman, with a jug in her hand, go into the kitchen; ſhe was occaſionally ſervant to the *Royal Family*, and the *Queen* was *pleaſed* TO BE THIRSTY.

CHAP.

CHAP. XII.

PATTERDALE.

Set off again to the Palace—Meet an old
Woman—Who she was—Enter into Con-
versation with her MAJESTY—*Some Gin*
—Her Majesty's Reasons for preferring
Ale—The Disaster that gave us the Ho-
nour of her Company—Complains of the
King—Her white Hand—Why she sup-
poses us rich—Her Poverty and Riches
—The King an old Fool—Observe the
King—Her Majesty abuses him—Wants
to sell two Wethers—The Queen get-
ting more fuddled—Her own Account
of her Behaviour at Church—She gets
worse and worse—The Parson of the
Parish.

AFTER *admiring* this *antiquated* maid
of honour, we had so violent an impulse
to

to fee the Royal Family, we immediately fet off to the Palace. We had not proceeded far before we met an old woman, with an earthen bottle in one hand, and a crooked ftick in the other; an old cloth (or what was once a *whole* handkerchief) was bound round her head, with dirty remnants of a gown. On her turning round, I thought of the " Old " Hag picking dry fticks and mumbling " to herfelf."——I had prepared my penny, when we were ftruck by a quick voice; " *A fine evening, gentlemen!*" Seeing the people leave their cottages, and the hay-makers lean over the gates, we concluded, and, not wrongfully, it was the Queen's betattered felf. We followed her to the public-houfe, and were furprized at our reception, though we had heard ftories that ought not to have made us fo. My friend entered into converfation with her majefty, when I felt myfelf fo emboldened by her gracious familiarity, I drew my chair towards her, and called for *fome gin.* I own myfelf

wrong

wrong in this, particularly as her majefty faid, fhe had not ate any thing for two days; and, although it was a favourite liquor, fhe would not tafte it; but faid, " I want fome ale to FEED my fto- " mach;" which proves it muft be very nourifhing, and that the DREGS, as one of our old poets calls them, turn to food.

I will not quote the couplet, though juft and natural, but go on to mention that fhe loudly complained *, " that " damned b——— Brunfcal † had put a " a fpider in my ale, and I could not " drink it, and be d— to her."——She defired the landlady to fill her bottle to take home with her, and then told us the

* Think not, reader, this is an imaginary chara¢ter, I introduce her very words. When a perfon is held up as a beacon, the delicate mind ought not to be fqueamifh at hearing immediate facts. Thofe who have the power of recolle¢tion fhould defcribe as they find, not as they wifh; and Truth, in a coarfe garb, may be a leffon to fome, though we may hope it will never be an example of imitation to any.

† Is not Brunfcal a good name for a maid of honour?

King

King had broke her hand and knee with his ftick ; this, we fufpected, was only, to fhew us as fair a hand, as any queen's whatever, difgraced by a filthy pair of woollen mittens curling half up her arms.—She faid, " her poverty was a "great grievance to her."—" But, I " fuppofe, as you have *rings* on your fin- " gers, you are very rich ; mayhap a thou- " fand a year." I had once a ring myfelf ; " but old Madam M—— always wore a " *golden one.*"—She then bridled up, and allowed fhe had *abundance* of money, and that fhe fpent a fhilling a day in drink, but very little in meat ; " and, to " be fure, I was very handfome when " young, and *not with child* when mar- " ried : I was a *bold* woman to venture " upon fo ftout a man as the king, but " he is now grown an old fool ;—but, I " tell you, Madam Dobfon, why don't " you bring me my ale, I called for it " half an hour ago ?"

Mrs,

Mrs. D—— knew what fhe meant, and went for a glafs, though fhe had not ordered it: fhe had fcarcely fwallowed the contents, before the king was obferved creeping towards the houfe. I could not help feeling refpect, he had fo fine a furrowed face, his head inclined towards the right fhoulder, with a ragged handkerchief tied under his chin, and his coat was much torn. He fat upon the table, and told her, with a feeble voice, he was come to take her home.—— She not only abufed him, but ftruck him twice, and then gave him a glafs out of her bottle to make amends.—I felt the utmoft indignation at her conduct, and brought him a chair; which he refufed, but feemed to take kindly, and, by way of acknowledgment, told me, " If you " chufe to buy a couple of FINE WE- " THERS*, you fhall have them very " cheap."

* They told us he did not keep any fheep, and they fuppofed he had received thefe wethers under his leafe

of

" cheap." This offer was too much for my rifible mufcles, and I laughed moft heartily.

The queen made fo many attacks upon her bottle, fhe became more noify, and fwore fhe had been drunk for two days ; " and as for going to church, I have not " been in one this feven years."—" Oh " yes, Madam, (faid the landlady) you " know you was when Mr. Myers " preached, and you *fmoked* your pipe in " church."—Oh ! d—— it, I recollect " that : he was preaching how we fhould " not only forgive a brother feven times, " but feventy times feven."—Her majefty rofe up in church, and told him, " I " have done it *a hundred times*, but no- " body minded me."

After every replenifh fhe increafed in noife. She was rather approaching too

of ENTERTAINMENTS.—See his character, Chapter XIV.

near,

near, and began to stroke the back of her hand acrofs her lips.: I heard this was a fymptom of kiffing; and blame me not, ye fair, for flying from the royal falute: I fwept round her, and left to another wight that honour.

We were now at tea, and fhe faid and fang fuch droll things, it burft through my nofe, and almoft choaked me. We perceived fhe was growing worfe; and as we had feen *quite* fufficient of Patter-dale royalty, we paid our bill, and made good our retreat.

While we were thus unaccountably aftonifhed, the parfon of the parifh went by, in a pair of clogs, a coloured coat, and blue worfted ftockings;—and with a large tree upon his fhoulder. The land-lord, who I have fince been informed was intended for the church, pointed him out to us.

CHAP.

CHAP. XIII.

Strength of Recollection—A Rush bearing.

WE returned the fame road we came, having only met two perfons in the morning. As we faw a man brufhing down a hill from a fteep flate quarry, we ftopped to afk fome queftions. My friend afked him if his name was not " Thomas Hayton :"—it was, but he did not prove to be the perfon he meant, though of the fame name. He afked him if he ufed to be a *ftage-player* * ?—" Aye, Sur, bu " that's

* My friend writes me this defcription of a ftage-player. " The cuftom of ftage-playing is very much " left off of late years ; I queftion whether any thing " now happens in fix or feven years. The plays they " formerly acted were, Cato, Barbaroffa, Taming the " Shrew ;

" that's above twenty years ago."—If you could have feen the man's face when my companion told him who he was, you muft have thought favourably of thefe mountaineers ; and I make no doubt but he muft have been a capital per-former. His colour changed, and he could fcarce fpeak ; and he at firft re-fufed the money offered him. After we had left him, he ftood for fome time like a ftatue, and then called after us, and told us, that an old man and his wife lived in the public-houfe below, that had once been *his* father's fervants.—We went to them, and I had the fatisfaction of finding my friend was as much be-loved when a boy, as he is now efteemed as a man. Scenes like thefe are in con-cord with a heart that wifhes well to all

" Shrew; much more in Tragedy than Comedy, as it
" had a greater effect upon the audience.—The per-
" formers were farmers' fons and farmers' fervants,
" by way of employment in long winter evenings,
" and at a time of the year when they had very little
" to do."

H   the

the world. I drew out my purfe; and was forry it was fo *thinly* ftocked.

How remarkable! for four people to meet in fo folitary a place, in the only houfe between Hartfop and Amblefide, in a diftant part of the country whence they all came, not having feen each other for thirty years!

The landlord, who was a *bit* of a far-mer, told us he wanted to look after fome fheep that fed upon a hill near our road. I could not help remarking with what fpeed the dog ran up the fkirts of the mountain, obedient to his call, and the motion of his hand. When the dog had done his duty, he barked down the hill, and came wagging his tail in much felf-approbation.

The old man then talked what *good fcholars* all his children were; and, by a hint of wifhing to get " *the fineft lad* " *'t h' world* provided for," I was con-vinced,

vinced, although he had not feen Mr.
—— for thirty years, he was informed
of the numbers he had befriended.

We fhook hands with the old man,
and then walked on, admiring the mountains around us, and over which evening
had thrown fo deep a fhade; we faw di-
vifions that were not vifible in the
morning; and when we reached the top
of Kirkftone, we had a partial fight of
the fea over Hawkefhead.

Our return was expeditious; the events
of the day were fine *antidotes* againft fatigue.

When we arrived at Amblefide, we
faw feveral garlands fupported by men
and little children, with a couple of fid-
dles; we made two in the throng, and
went to fee them planted in the church.
Two young ladies graced the pulpit, and
I never faw a fairer parfon and clerk in
my life; that's of *courfe* you know, for

it

it was too dark to judge. I was forry
to obferve many men came in with hats
on : it certainly was not in the original
inftitution ; but they, perhaps, thought
Night would cover every thing.

This is an old Roman catholic cuftom, though without any fuperftitious
remains. Againft the next Sunday the
old rufhes that have ferved a year are
removed, and the clerk is allowed *a fmall
fum* to fupply frefh-gathered ones.

CHAP.

CHAP. XIV.

THE KING OF PATTERDALE.

*His great Age—Supposed why called so—
Astonishing Accumulation of Wealth—
Mode of trying strength of Ponies—Cast
away on an uninhabited Island—Contri-
vance to eat his Victuals, without his Af-
sistant knowing he had any—His peculiar
Mode of letting Fields, &c.—Partiality
for Sugar—Only out-cunninged in his
Amours—Excellent Character of his Son
—His Majesty's Reasons for not giving to
the Poor—The Queen offers her Granddaughter in Marriage—Respect paid to
her by the Country People.*

I FEEL myself at a loss to give a character of his majesty. I have every pos-
sible respect for his advanced age; but

H 3   the

the meanness of the miser hinders me
from paying it.

He is now in his 93d year, and had a
paternal eſtate of from 150*l.* to 200*l.* a
year, which has always given the (imaginary) title of *King of Patterdale* to its
poſſeſſor : it is ſaid, from being formerly
exonerated from ſome particular tax,
which might be owing to its very *remote*
ſituation, and not worth gathering.

By his niggardly parſimonioufneſs he
has realized his fortune, according to
ſome, to 600*l.* by many to 800*l.* a year ;
and I have even heard him ſaid to be
worth 40,000*l.*—A ſtrong conſtitution
gave him an opportunity of being laborious, and his induſtry kept pace with
his deſire of gain. He knew to omit getting one ſhilling was a certain loſs of
one penny a year for ever, beſides com-
pound intereſt, that accumulating con-
ſideration to THE MISERS of the day.

He

He had many ponies that he kept upon the common land, which he was entitled to from his landed property in the parifh : upon thefe *lean,* beafts he carried his own charcoal over the mountains to the different forges ; he ufed to throw his hat in their faces to fee if they were able to perform the journey ; thofe that did not mind the hat were lucky enough to remain at home, and thofe which ran afide, were thought of fufficient ftrength.

This may ferve as an example to thofe who keep unfortunate animals, and furnifh a new mode of trying if they have any ftrength left : I recommend this to Bunbury, for his next edition of " GAM-" BADO."

He was reckoned the beft boatman between Patterdale and Dunmallart Head; and he ufed to convey his own flate and wood ; or, when other people wanted him, for a trifling fum *per* load. He

H 4   was

was once deeply laden with the latter, and was driven by a violent gale of wind upon the largeſt iſland *. In this ſituation he remained with his aſſiſtant two days. The poor fellow, expecting a ſhort paſſage, had made no proviſion ; his majeſty always carried bread and cheeſe in his pocket to avoid going to ale-houſes, although he was never known to refuſe, when he was offered *to be treated*. When he wanted to eat, he told the man he would go to the other ſide of the iſland to ſee if the wind was likely to change ; he then *gormandized* away, and made the man believe he had only been to look after the weather.

I muſt now mention a cuſtom he has long practiſed, which ſaves him the expence of providing meals at home :— to uſe his own words, he calls them

---

* On theſe lakes the wind ſometimes gathers round the hills, and has a violent effect: There has lately been a loaded boat and two men loſt on Windermere.

7

" EN-

" ENTERTAINMENTS." He lets fome fields and fmall houfes, as expreffed in the agreement, for fo many dinners and fuppers, taking care that what are to him dainties are provided for each feparate day.

In his tea-drinkings, he takes from ten to fourteen cups, ufing an immoderate quantity of fugar, of which he is fo fond, he generally carries fome loofe in his pocket ; if he omits a day, which was once rarely the cafe, it is looked upon as fulfilled.—I am told it was a hard bargain to his tenants, but his great age has rather turned in their favour.

There are numberlefs ftories of him, throughout the country, in which his cunning was always confpicuous, and only *in his amours* has he been (fometimes) over-reached. Thefe are more funny to hear than it would be decent to relate.

I have

I have not exceeded a tittle in what I heard of this patriarch mifer ; and I am the more induced to write about him, becaufe I could not learn, he had ever performed one act of charity, throughout a life, that Providence has lengthened beyond the ufual ftage of man.

Though " the ways of heaven are " dark and intricate," they are always juft.

Perhaps this man is held up, as *a beacon,* to thofe who might otherwife be mifers, for I never faw people that appear lefs inclined to be fo than thofe around him ; and his fon is a confpicuous example of the contrary. Brought up in a peculiar manner, his benevolent character fhines a juft contraft ; and the inhabitants fay, when he gets poffeffion of the fortune, charity to the poor will be as diffufive in the richeft man in Patterdale as fordidnefs is now. The king allows

lows he never got any thing by the
poor; why then fhould he give them
any thing? He fometimes has been
heard to complain, that a man fhould
be cut off in the prime of his life, at
eighty or ninety years—if he could live
to the age of Methufalem, he might fave
a little money!

The queen is many years younger than
he is, but keeps pace with him in his
paffion for money. She offered her
granddaughter in marriage to my friend,
and faid, " the old rafcal fhould give
" him 3000l. aye, guineas if he pleafed."
After fo great an offer, I had the curiofity to afk her for a glafs of ale; but
fhe had too much her bottle at heart,
and turned it off with a fong. They
told us fhe was often more difguftful than
when we faw her; for it was one of her
MODERATE fits of drinking.

I mentioned before, the maid of honour only occafionally waits upon them;
and

and the young one we faw at the palace belongs to the fon.

Notwithftanding the queen behaved fo remarkably, fome countrymen, who came to hear the fun, and the people of the houfe, always called her " *Madam M———.*" They took care fhe fhould not fee them laughing at her, and always fpoke in a tone of refpect.

Such power has that *idol* wealth on the minds of misjudging mortals.

CHAP.

CHAP. XV.

THE ASCENT OF HELM CRAG.

As the Subject of this Chapter is new to the Author, he chuses to say nothing more about it, but that he deals somewhat in Surmise; and he leaves the Decision to more learned Heads.

WE went in the morning to Graffmere church. There was a very decent congregation. The finging was old-fafhioned and good; and, if it had not been for a certain twang at the beginning of every ftave, I fhould have thought them amongft the beft country fingers I have heard. The men fat on one fide of the aile, the women on the other, upon rough oak benches; and I could not help obferving *the fmiles* interchanged when a couple were afked in marriage.

After

After as good and well-dreſſed a dinner, at Robert Newton's, as man could
wiſh, we ſet out to ſurmount the ſteep
aſcent of Helm Crag; but the dinner
was ſo cheap, I muſt mention what it
conſiſted of:

    Roaſt pike, ſtuffed,
    A boiled fowl,
    Veal-cutlets and ham,
    Beans and bacon,
    Cabbage,
    Peaſe and potatoes,
    Anchovy ſauce,
    Parſley and butter,
    Plain butter,
    Butter and cheeſe,
    Wheat bread and oat cake,
Three cups of preſerved gooſeberries,
with a bowl of rich cream in the centre:
    For two people, at ten-pence a head.

We went up a narrow lane, that gave
us, half a mile from the church, a new
                        view

view of Graffmere valley, with a perpetual water-fall, juftly, from its force,
called *White-churn Gill.* It rufhes from
a crefcent-heathed hill, and forms one
of the moft confiderable brooks that fupplies Graffmere.

The fun was hot ; and, after a gentle
afcent of about a mile, we refted fome
minutes under a thick hawthorn, which
we call the foot of the Crag.—The projecting point of the firft rife looked formidable ; and not lefs fo, to fpeak in
plain Englifh, from having a complete
belly-full : however, when people are
determined to overcome difficulties, time
and circumftances are no obftructions.

We were covered from the wind ; and
it was fo fteep, we were frequently obliged to ftop when we met a narrow
fhelf, and when we got to the firft range
of the hill I was glad to throw myfelf
down, panting for relief. The grafs was
flippery, which we guarded againft by

2   forcing

forcing our fticks as deep into the ground as we poffibly could ; and, when we had gained the feccond height, I never re member meeting a more cheerful relief, than finding we had got over that part of the hill which kept the wind from us. This not only enlivened us, but we opened upon profpects, which promifed to repay our labour when we had fur-mounted it.

The pinnacle hanging over our right obliged us to take a fweep; but, as we had the wind and a near fight of the top, we found lefs trouble in this ftage than in the others. We were exactly one hour from the hawthorn, which was not from its being a high hill, but the fteep-eft in this part of the country, being fel-dom frequented but by foxes, fheep, and ravens. Our guide was never on it but once; and neither he, nor Partridge, re-members that it has been vifited by ftrangers.

But

But I muſt be allowed to reſt myſelf a little before I ſay any thing of the proſpects around, and while I look with awful pleaſure at the ſight.

We went upon the projecting pinnacle, which had juſt room to hold two, from which I mark the views ; but I thought it prudent to have a leſs exalted ſtation in order to write them down.

The ſummit is covered with pieces of rock that give it the features of a grand ruin, occaſioned by an earthquake, or a number of ſtones jumbled together after the myſtical manner of the Druids. There is a deep fiſſure, two feet broad and twenty long, with a ſtone over one end of it, giving it the look of a ſtep over a mill-ſtream. Although I am not verſed in antiquities, I cannot help thinking this fiſſure reſembles the *Kiſtvaens* of the Druids, as deſcribed by Captain Groſe *.

* In his Preface, p. 136.

I   I wiſh

I wifh fome antiquary would inveftigate
this mountain. I think his fellow la-
bourers would be obliged to him; at any
rate, if he does not find fufficient to au-
thenticate my furmife, he will have fuch
delightful views around him, as will repay him for his trouble, and, I truft,
may induce him to think he has not
taken this labour in vain.

By dropping a fmall ftone down a
rent, you hear it rebound a long time.
One bending-ftone ferves as a fhelter for
fheep, where we found a mufhroom, the
only one we faw in the North. May not
this ftone, from its bend, be a part of
the *Cromleh* of the Druids?

The circumference, including its mis-
fhapen points, may be above a mile; and
where there is any foil, the grafs is fhort
and fweet. From this unfrequented fummit we faw the whole of Windermere.
Efthwaite water, and by Graffmere, being our point, they made a complete tri-
angle,

angle, divided by rich paftures, &c. whilft the valley, and its appendages, directly under us, feemed to contain every thing that can be beautiful in rural miniature.

We overlooked the Tarn, whence White-churn Gill has its fource, inclofed in a heath horfe fhoe, whofe fides were moft brilliantly befpangled with fmooth ftones, occafioned by a thin fheet of wa-ter oozing over them, and an almoft perpendicular fun.

We obferved over Helvellyn and the Grain of Seat Sandal a torrent of rain, whilft over Bownefs and to the South-eaft it was collecting fo partially, the diftance gave them the appearance of water-fpouts. We imagined we had nothing to fear from any of them; it was clear over us; and, in the quarter whence the wind blew, the guide had fcarcely faid fo, ere we obferved the clouds from Seat Sandal pufhing againft

I 2   the

the wind, though they were confiderably exhaufted on thofe mountains. We were foon convinced of our ill-judging, and took fhelter in the fheep-cove, which, by bending, held us fecure. This was too confined a fituation ; and as the rain had fomewhat ceafed, the guide and I went about one hundred and fifty yards down the hill. The rain came on, and wet me to the fkin ; but we were amply repaid by the moft luminous fight I ever beheld, and which I fhall attempt to de-fcribe.

The fun fhone with fuch brilliancy through flanting drops, they looked like a line of cryftal as round as a finger, and there was a fpray intermixed, variegated as a rainbow. Newton, who has been all his life accuftomed to mountains, fays he never faw any thing like it before. Might not it be owing to the dark heath over the Tarn, and a partial fhining of the fun upon the Crag ?

Too

Too much rain had fallen to render the grafs lefs flippery. We were obliged to traverfe down the hill with the utmoft caution, and, if not with the difficulty of the afcent, with confiderable more danger. When we opened Seat Sandal, we were furprized by a fuperb cataract, occafioned by the rain which fell whilft we were upon the fummit.

I could not help expecting and wifhing we could have had a thunder ftorm.

Let the confiderate mind contemplate on the various fights prefented to us in fo fhort a fpace.

CHAP.

CHAP. XVI.

Coniſtone Lake—Reaſons for thinking a Man
a Guide—The old Man—Impulſe to viſit
it—Repent—The old Gentleman's moſſy
Cloathing—Sheep—A Spring—Views
diſcernible—Eaſy Deſcent—Leven's Caſ-
cade—Walk up a Caſemate—Copper
Works—Slate Quarry—A Volcano—
Afraid to viſit it—A young Man attempts,
and ſwoons—His Manner to avoid being
laughed at—Superſtition—Full a Match
for Robin Partridge's—Ghoſts—Whiſt-
ling a Charm againſt them.

BY my propoſal it was intended we
ſhould paſs an idle morning; but the
day was ſo fine, we ſet off to Coniſtone
Lake, purpoſing to take Hawkeſhead on
our return.

We

We paſſed round the head of Windermere, and aſcended many brows, ſeeing
mountains we did not know, and recollecting others we had viſited. We had
likewiſe an irregular ſight of Eſthwaite
water. The road is chiefly bounded by
heath, and you catch many pleaſing
views, which cannot help ſtriking the
eye with novelty wherever it wanders.

From a purple hill, at the head of
Coniſtone Lake, you have a full view
of it. The borders are well wooded, but
they have not that livelineſs of paſture
which adorns Windermere.

Whilſt we were making obſervations, a
man in his harveſt dreſs, with a pair of
handſome ſpectacles on (an unuſual ſight
for one in his ſtation) ſeated himſelf near
us; and we were ſoon convinced, by
certain ſhrewd remarks, and proud ex-
preſſions of the ſuperior beauty of Coniſtone Lake, that he wiſhed to officiate

I 4   as

as guide; and, upon his particularly pointing to a high mountain called the OLD MAN, fymptoms appeared of wifh- ing to afcend it. We did not ftop to hefitate; but we had the precaution to take fome brandy, and at one o'clock began the arduous tafk.

I often repented during two hours toil, and was almoft inclined to give it up; but that would have difgraced my former bravadoes. My companion kept the ftart of me; and when I reached the fummit, he was placing ftones on three heaps, called the *Old Man*, his *Wife*, and *Son*, where there had once been a bea- con. As foon as I was fomewhat re- covered, and had time to look about me, I was charmed to find the Old Gentle- man crowned with the deepeft mofs I had ever trod upon, and that he could boaft of a head beautifully fweeping about half a mile in length, and a quar- ter in breadth, rifing in one part like the bofom of a great wave. Numbers
of

of sheep were gamboling about, as if they were inclined to shew their superior agility. We soon came to a bulging spring. I knelt down ; drank copiously of as soft and cool water as I ever tasted ; and did not forget a mental recollection to the health, of the whole race of human beings around me. I had the precaution, however, to prepare my stomach for the luxurious beverage, by a gulp of brandy.

The day was rather unfavourable ; but we had sometimes extensive views, with a fine sight of the sea beyond Lancaster, in which quarter the heavens were the most favourable ; but we were not so lucky as to see Scotland and the Isle of Man, which, we were told, were sometimes very visible. We counted a dozen pieces of water, most of them on the summit of hills. The guide pointed to a pond considerably above the level of the sea, in which char in full roe have been put. The old ones are grown lank and

and poor, but the breed are fmall and fweet-flavoured. Another pond is full of ill-tafted trout and perch, fo badly fupplied with food from the upper hills, that they always bite greedily. We were in the clouds, which were flying the fwifteft rate I ever faw—almoft as fwift as thought.

After lightly treading over the length of the height, we defcended on the fame front; and, although fteep, it was perfectly fafe, from the depth of mofs.

About one-third of the way, we came to a deep tarn, called Leven's water, which occafions an enchanting waterfall, and fupplies the copper-works with water. When we reached the embouchure of the fall, I got upon a rock, and have the pleafure of expreffing what I felt:—It rufhes out with fuch force, it gives a bow of water an elevation of twenty degrees, then fpreads down the rocks; to the right of the mouth, there

is

is a point againſt which it daſhes in vain, and number of cryſtal balls are forced over it, which made me think (if I may be allowed the expreſſion) of a Liliputian bombardment.

I had the curioſity to go two hundred yards up a funnel, half-leg deep in water, expecting it was a copper mine. In this I was diſappointed; there was but one Cyclops at work, who was engaged in opening a communication, or, in the technical terms of mining, in driving a level to the other ſide of the brook, to draw off the obſtructing waters from the mine. He ſhewed us ſome copper, mingled with the rock, which is ſo ſparingly mixed, it is not worth the expence of ſeparating.

The mine is at preſent rather barren; but this mountain has been ſo productive, they do not doubt meeting with ſuccefs; and they already keep ſome men at work, though not in proportion to the expences. We deſcended lower, where

they

they pulverized it, and, by different pro-
ceffes, were preparing it for fmelting,
which is carried on in a country better
fupplied with coal, and more convenient
for navigation. ·

Our excurfion was performed in four
hours and a half, and by a little after
nine we were again at head quarters.

There are feveral flate quarries upon
this mountain.   I looked in at one near
the fummit ; there is a gallery to it, and
it is arched like an immenfe Gothic roof.

A copper mine, in Elizabeth's days,
was worked by Government, and produced great profit. The guide pointed to a part where there has been a volcano, and offered to take us to the mouth
of it; he fhewed us fome honeycomb-lava
he had got from it. We had too much
labour before us, or it was too hazardous
for me to undertake. He told us of a
little gentleman that went up with him

laft

laft year, who boafted that he could venture up any precipice; but, before they
reached the mouth, his head gave way,
and he fainted.   He had much toil and
danger in dragging him down; and
when they had arrived at a fafe part, he
bribed him not to expofe him to his
party, who were given to underftand he
had performed the arduous tafk, particularly (if I recollect right) as the guide
gave him a piece of lava to keep as a
trophy of his boldnefs.

I am told, Coniftone Lake deferves
more attention than we had time to pay
to it.   Chreighton, the guide, is a felf-
taught fcholar, and will want few hints
to give you a copious account of every
thing in his neighbourhood.   He faid
fomething about his being a defcendant
of a noble family in Scotland, and feemed
inclined to be very diffufe in fpeaking of
great people; but, as it was not for us
to trouble our heads about them, we
paffed them quickly over.

One

One of the handed-down ſtories of credulity, which I dare ſay half the people believe, is of an old man who became rich, his neighbours knew not how; though ſome ſay he had a copper mine in the mountain. He was often deſired to tell how he got his riches, and one fatal evening he told them the *devil* had aſſiſted him in getting his copper, but mark the reſult; the next time he went up the hill, he was found torn to pieces; and, though he probably fell down a precipice, the good folks will have it, the *devil* killed him, out of revenge, for betraying his ſecrets.

. People in theſe remote parts tell ſuch kind of ſtories very gravely, and there is hardly an old barn that has not had a ghoſt in ſome ſhape or other; but, as we never hear of any one being frightened out of his ſenſes, they are very *harmleſs* kind of ghoſts, and you have no reaſon

to

7

to be afraid of them; as thefe aërials generally perform their fantaftics at night: *whiftling* is the charm, and, when a man approaches a place famous for their haunts, he increafes his *Lillebulero* powers.

CHAP.

CHAP. XVII.

*A Peep into Troutbeck Dale—All defcrip-
tive ; if you don't chufe to read it, let it
alone—But take a Walk to it, and if you
meet the fame pretty Girl and obliging
Perfon we did, fo much the better.*

WE went round a hanging wood *,
paffed the foot of it ; then turned up a
lane, which gave a noble command of
the Rydal hills. Afcending about four
hundred yards we fee Dove Neft, and,
for the firft time, obferve it has turreted
wings. A little higher we croffed a dou-
ble-trunked afh, and had a view of the
lake, comprehending Belle-Ifland. On-
wards Croft Houfe appeared in virgin

---

* The high road below Low Wood.

neat-

neatnefs, under fhade of a hill that was
foon to cover it from us.

We then advanced about a mile,
which brought us to the only gate acrofs
the lane, and, by looking over the wall,
have a bold view of Calgarth, beautified
by woods, on each fide a new-making
avenue, with a winding canal to Windermere.

It is from this fpot we have a moft enchanting command, and I will venture
to think the trueft fight of the lake.
Belle-ifle houfe, as an object, is entirely
loft, and appears, fince we know its fite,
the largeft tree on the ifland. The left
prefents us with floping hills, terminated
by a table mountain : and, by taking a
peep under fome oak boughs, to the
right, we juft take in the cap of our yefterday's friend, the Old Man.

We proceeded over the vale of Troutbeck, where the modeft manfion of

K

Judge

Judge Wilſon *, the church, and the village, became pretty objects. The vale is quiet and intereſting, with a brook running through it, well ſupplied with ſweet trout.

* Since this was written, the publick have been deprived of the abilities of this excellent Judge, by a paralytic ſtroke, for which he had in vain ſought relief at Liſbon. He died at Kendal ; where the following elegant tribute to his memory, from the pen of the Biſhop of Landaff, has ſince been placed :

" In memory of
Sir JOHN WILSON, Knight,
one of his Majeſty's Juſtices of the
Court of Common Pleas.
Born at the Howe in Applethwaite,
6th of Auguſt, 1741.
Died at Kendal, 18th of October, 1793.
He did not owe his promotion
to the weight of
great connexions, which he never courted ;
nor to the influence of
political parties, which he never joined :
but to his profeſſional merit,
and the unſolicited patronage of the
Lord Chancellor Thurlow,
who, in recommending to his Majeſty
ſo profound a lawyer,
and ſo good a man,
realized the hopes and expectations of
the whole Bar,
gratified the wiſhes of the Country,
and did honour to
his own diſcernment and integrity."

Being

Being at a lofs how to proceed, we enquired from a pretty girl what turning
we were to take. She told us to go up
any lane to the left, and we muft crofs
over fome ftone walls, and that fhe was
going after fome fheep, and fhould *keep
an eye* after us, to fce if we kept the
right road. This ruftic civility, fo un-
affectedly pleafing, was rendered ufelefs,
by our meeting a well-dreffed perfon, who
faid he was going to Amblefide, and
offered to take us a pleafant round.

We returned by the Troutbeck Hundred; and had a full view of the lake, a
table hill, and a fight of Millthorp Sands.
We wound above Dove Neft, in the feparation between High Wood and Low,
and had a comprehenfive fight of the
Rathay, winding into the lake, with
Ballam tarn over fome high wood that
divides it from the head of Windermere.

Such was our morning's excurfion of
three hours and a half.

K 2   CHAP

CHAP. XVIII.

AMBLESIDE WATERFALL.

A Copy of Verfes, introduced to fhew you I am no defpicable Poet ; but, as Poetry is a Drug, turn to the next Leaf, and you will find I got a bad Tumble, with Advice to guard againft fuch Difafters.

AS we have feen moft of the diftant views about this neighbourhood, we got up early, and went to a cafcade a little mile from the houfe. After going through the inn yard, we afcended along the fteep banks of a brook. The firft fight of the cafcade comprehends the three parts as in one; it is more interefting than any we have hitherto feen, from being partially hid by over-hanging trees, and a rocky, yet verdant, ifland, which

fepa-

feparates the upper fall, and makes two
diftinct flufhes, meeting at a point of the
ifland in a bafin.

Advance one hundred yards, and feat
yourfelf (if you can look down a-fmall
precipice) in an oak that juts over it,
which is fafe, and well guarded with
many trunks bound with ivy.

It was here I recollected fome verfes
I once wrote under a Banian tree *, that
reminded me of the fterling oak.

* A tree fo fond of itfelf, it takes root from its
branches, and in time becomes a monftrous fize. This
tree was in DUM DUM gardens, in the vicinity of Cal-
cutta, near an annual encampment of as fine a body of
men, with fome as pleafant and good officers as ever
ferved their country; many of whom have fince loft their
lives, nobly fighting in its fervice.

K 3

On

ON CONSTANCY *.

When kindred hearts together join,
And like the oak and ivy twine,
　　How bleſt the happy pair!
But, ſhould the oak receive a wound,
Is not the tendril ivy found
　　To feel an equal ſhare?
Such hearts as theſe with union feelings glow;
And, turning, tremble at — or joy — or woe.

THE SIMILE.

The oak is man in firmneſs dreſt,
With ſtrength of fondneſs in his breaſt,
　　Delighting in the tie!
The ivy is the gentle wife,
That clings around his happy life
　　With deathleſs conſtancy;
In LIFE ſhe does her folding joys impart,
In DEATH ſhe withers round the ſapieſs HEART,

* See Gentleman's Magazine for November, 1788.

But

But to return; here you divide the
ifland, and when you are fufficiently lull-
ed, caft your eyes downwards, and you
will fee the mountain afh fhewing its red
berries amidft variegated verdure ; on
reaching the head of it, you will obferve fome large ftones, which occafion
the divifion. The hanging ifland has an
enchanting effect, and, I think, looks
more interefting than the old bridge at
the loweft fall at Rydal, becaufe one is
the effect of chance, and the other of
order. Let not the flying traveller think
it too laborious to walk up to this enchanting ifland.

And you, ye fair ! that cannot venture
upon mountains, tread cautioufly by the
fide of this mufical rivulet, and you will
be repaid by fo impreffive a fight as can
never be eradicated from memory—a
fight calculated to remind you of the
fofteft moments of your life.

K 4   The

The ſtones were ſo wet and ſlippery I got a clumſy tumble. I mention this, as it was the firſt time I went out without a ſtick, and I would adviſe thoſe who go up hills to have one.

CHAP.

CHAP. XIX.

The Weſtons—A Song to rock a Cradle by
—Hawkeſhead—An Epitaph calculated
to remind us of the Inſtability of human
Life—School Boys, a noble Sight—Cheap-
neſs of Boarding—A good School—A
Debt of Honour—A Paſtoral Dinner—
People who live ſo—Fine Stocks for fine
Children—The Rathay and the Brathay
—Haymakers at Dinner.

AFTER giving the waterfall we have
juſt ſeen conſiderably the preference to
the others, we ſet off to Hawkeſhead,
which commands Eſtwaite water. We
croſſed two fine old bridges over the
Rathay and the Brathay, ſeparating
Weſtmoreland from Lancaſhire. The
firſt river has two arches over it, and
runs

runs ftrong. The laft is facing a good houfe, where the infamous Gilberts, alias Weftons, concealed themfelves, fo noted for their robberies and forgeries, and fince executed. Thefe bad men had the knack of gaining the regard of the poor people, kept moft excellent horfes, and hunted with the neighbouring gentlemen.

The Brathay has an ifland near the bridge, and has a mill-pond appearance until it glides towards Windermere, joining the Rathay, and making a handfome entrance into the lake. We then took the upper road until we came to a poor cottage, where a girl was rocking a cradle: I afked her to give me fome whey.—" I'll *gi hoa fum*, if you'll *rok th'* " *cradle a bit* ;"—a tafk I readily undertook, to the tune of " *Hufh, my dear, lie ftill and flumber.*"

We very foon came to Belmont, belonging to the Rev. Mr. Braithwaite, which

which is a very handfome houfe, and the
grounds about it well laid out. We
counted in one field fifty turkeys, including two or three broods; and the land
feems to have a good farmer for its owner. He has a fweet view of Eaft-
waite water, the white-wafhed town of
Hawkefhead, and the church. The hills
around are fmall, but beautifully variegated.

The town of Hawkefhead has a good
market-place, and it is endowed with a
free-fchool, where upwards of one hundred boys are at prefent educated. We
went into the church-yard, and faw Belmont in fine view, with a very commanding fight of the lake. The beauty
of the church is much enhanced by being white, and having a row of windows over the firft roof; a contraft with
the blue flating, that has a picturefque
effect.

After

After viewing the church, which is not remarkable for cleanlinefs, I took down the following epitaph :

" To the Memory of
" Robert Benfon, and Sarah his wife,
" of this parifh.
" He died 19th Feb. 1750, aged 90 years.
" She died 16th Nov. 1769, aged 97.
" They had four fons and fix daughters
" that lived to be men and women ; of
" whom feven attended their mother to
" the grave, whofe ages made together
" 450 years. Their fon John, late of
" London, merchant, caufed this plate
" to be erected."

Of the feven who attended their mother's funeral there is only one remaining, and fhe is between eighty and ninety. This leffon of longevity and mortality is finely calculated to remind us of the inftability of human life.

I

The

The school-boys, whose ruddy cheeks prove the healthfulness of the situation, were in clusters on the hill. I cannot conceive a more pleasing sight than these young heroes made; amongst the number was a youth we had seen (all life) at Levens. He seemed to have a tear of recollection. As this was the first day after holidays, and the sight of us reminded him of his friends, it was not to be wondered at.—To shew you what a charming creature Nature is, we did not say ten words to him at Levens; but, as he had seen us in a place he liked, we became *a part* of it, and he remained close to us as long as he could. —If Lavater had seen this boy in the two lights we did, he would have said, he has the life of a boy of spirit, tempered with sensibility.

There are many boarding-houses for the boys, and, including washing, the expences do not exceed fourteen pounds a year. The head master has the credit

of

of fending out fome moft excellent fcholars; and was expected home this day,
from the perambulations he ufually takes
during vacation-time.

On our return, we took the loweft and
the neareft road, but went a little out
of our way to pay *a debt of honour* we
had promifed to the girl that gave us
fome whey. The family was at dinner,
and confifted of a young couple with
three children, the eldeft not three years
old. The cradle was ftill going, tied by
a long ftring to the father's * chair, who
rocked with one hand whilft he ate with
the other. They feemed to have lufty
appetites; their paftoral fare confifted
of oat cakes, cheefe, and butter; their
beverage butter-milk and whey.

When we went away, my friend overheard the wife fay, " Whau dun yaw think

* I have heard with concern, the once induftrious
father is dead.

" they

" they are ?" It is fuch ftocks as thefe that furnifh our warriors, our weavers, and hufbandmen, and by the fwcat of their brows keep it from the idle.

We fhould readily have joined the party, and partook with them; but there did not feem fo much plenty as peace, and we left them with our beft wifhes.

Upon an old quarry on the firft common, fhaped like a battery, with two embrafures, and oppofite the head of Ballam Tarn, are four floping fields full of cattle and fheep. The left gives four interfected fights of Windermere; and I dare venture to recommend it as a fituation capable of fhewing the varied beauties of the lake; befides, it is a good refting-place for walkers. We have likewife Low Wood, and are fo directly in the centre of that foliaged hill, the fummit refembles the Peak of Teneriffe *;

---

* The author once faw the fun rifing upon the Peak, in wonderful grandeur.

and

and Amblefide mountain fhews its BIG BELLY as if it was proud of its pof-feffions.

From Brathay bridge, Loughrig Fell rifes in a ridge of clumps that appear as if they were running a race until they form a point, which prefents another face from the window where I am wri-ting, well wooded and watered, and compofes part of the valley that is our head quarters.

This valley is a moft refrefhing fight after a fatiguing walk of fix hours, fuch as we have had, without a breath of air: but even this prefented fomething new; for, when we looked down the lake, every objeét was in refleétion, and I thought it the cleareft mirrour I ever faw. But my MUSE fhall fpeak for me; and you are to fuppofe the verfes were written at the head of Windermere.

The

The glorious ORB, that gilds th' unequall'd whole,
Enforces rev'rence on th' enraptur'd foul ;
Or ſtrikes with *dimneſs* the preſuming eye,
That meets his journey through the placid ſky ;
But what he cheers with wond'ring mind we view,
And, gazing round, find beauties ever new.

The lowing herds with diſtant caſcades join ;
The bleating ſheep with tinkling founds combine ;
The *choral* * brooks, moſt muſical and near,
In fulleſt harmony delight the ear ;
From wood to hill, from crag to fertile vales,
Melodious echos ! tell their plaintive tales ;
With varied ſpeed, through ſightleſs caverns ſtray,
And, in the peaceful valleys, die away.

No playful zephyrs the rich foliage ſhake,
Or curl the quiet boſom of the lake ;
The trees, the crags, and the high-tufted ſteep,
Reflect their beauties on the MIRROIR deep.
The azure ſoftneſs of a cloudleſs ſky
Tints on the ſurface—a celeſtial dye ;
And, when through op'nings of wild verdure ſeen,
Adorns the ſhade of Nature's liberal green.
The little cot, that on the margin ſtands,
An equal thatch in the bright lake commands.

———

* Not very diſtant from the conjoining of the Rathay
and Brathay, the feeders of the Lake.

L   The

The sheep, in clusters, underneath the shade,
In the dun umbrage of the deep are laid;
Or, as they stray upon the daisied grass,
The stragglers glide along the liquid glass.
Scenes such as these the veteran Walkers cheer,
Toil is forgot,—Contentment dwelleth near.
The busy hay-folks *, earlier than the sun,
Quit not their labour when his course is done;
And many a time, on such a cloudless day,
At morn 'twas herbage what at night is hay;
Stor'd in their household granaries away.
Oh! what delight! where rural quiet reigns!
'Tis peace to man, and plenty to the plains;
Bloom to the Fair, gives candour to the young,
Health to the old, and mildness to the strong.
Be wise, ye Villagers! quit not your homes;
He ne'er gains comfort, that for LUCRE roams.
Envy and Pride attend the road to wealth;
Labour and Peace, to innocence and health.

For us—with humbled minds we gaze around,
Until we fancy 'tis enchanted ground;
Presumption thus, from the charm'd bosom driv'n,
And ALL is full—of NATURE and of HEAV'N.

———

* The grass is so fine, that, in a day like this, what
was cut in the morning is often housed in the evening.

We

We were this day agreeably entertained on feeing fome hay-makers at dinner. " The loud laughs befpoke their " vacant minds ;" and, though they were at a confiderable diftance, we could hear every word, echo is fo diftinct in thefe valleys. I heard one man fay, " I tell " thee, I will kifs thee, Molly."—" Tha " fhant," was the anfwer ; but we faw him do it—and heard the fmack too.

L 2 CHAP.

CHAP. XX.

Roman Station—A large Frog—Charity—
Character of a good Man.

WHILST my friend went upon Loughrig Fell, Mr. Kellet, the perfon who
fhewed us civility at Troutbeck, took
me towards Water head, where there
has once been a Roman ftation *, but
which is now more ufefully covered with
good grafs, barley, and oats. Adjoining is an old barn, built from the ftones
taken from the pavement.

The road is not more than fix yards
wide, until it reaches High-ftreet, which

* No ftation could be better calculated for a large
body of men; at no great diftance from the fea, with
frefh water near the fpot; interfecting many roads, and
every hill has a command over an app·oach to it.

is fix miles off, upon the top of a hill; it is then near twelve yards broad, and continues that width a mile and a half.

I vifited the caufeway with refpect to the once lords of it, and took up a large ftone from a part made bare to afcertain its breadth.   In doing this, I difturbed a large frog, that feemed full-blown with Roman pride ; and I replaced its *antient caftellum.*

Roman remains are often found ; and two years ago an urn full of coin was dug up.

If to-morrow turns out favourable, we purpofe mounting Helvellyn, and or-dering a chaife to meet us—as we think it proper to enter upon a new ftation with a dafh, and that too often claims attention.

As we are going to leave Amblefide, it is but juftice to the neighbouring gen-

L 3   tlemen

tlemen to fay the poor fpeak of them with much affection.

One gentleman, they fay, is rather given to " cholers" and " rages :" but they always like to fee him in them; for he never fcolds any one, but foon afterwards either gives or fends a mark of his bounty; as a poor man told us, " Why, " furs! I dun aw believe there's a more ge- " nerofity mon in aw th' world than he is."

They are very partial to colonel T——, who, through life, has been remarkable for liberality of mind, and who with a fmall fortune does all the good he can. An inftance that happened this morning will verify the reft. My companion overheard him afking the landlord if he had room for all his hay; on his faying he had not, he told him he would give him the ufe of one of his barns. When Providence beftows plentiful crops, how lucky it is to have a neighbour, who is

equally

equally confiderate in time of plenty as charitable in fcarcity !

I would have done myfelf the honour of paying my refpects to this gentleman, in return for the attention he had formerly paid to fome of my family ; but it would have broke through our original plan : for, as we had travelled upwards of four hundred miles purpofely to fee the Lakes, it would have been idle to have gone either to the right or to the left, when it would interfere with our giving up our whole time to them.

If this fhould fall into his hands, he may recollect me from this remark. I am one of the two perfons fpoken of through his neighbourhood for their long perambulations ; and I would wifh him to receive this as a proof of my knowledge of, and efteem for, his character.

L 4   CHAP.

CHAP. XXI,

HELVELLYN.

Full Moon—Courfe to Helvellyn—Difficult Undertaking—Views—Violent Thirft—A Tarn—Diffuaded from drinking.—A narrow Hill—Baffenthwaite Lake.

IMPATIENT for the morn, I rofe between three and four, and faw we had a clear fky. The full moon was juft going to drop over the very point of Loughrig Fell, and tinged all around it with folemnity. I was in the midft of the fcene, when my friend (always punctual to his time) fent me a candle, with notice that he was ready. I did not permit him to wait long, and before four o'clock we fet off.

We

We began our courfe by Rydal Hall,
guided by Robin Partridge; and, as we
furmounted the firft hills, took advantage of the morning to exert ourfelves.
We did not fee the fun rife, but obferved
with pleafure its fide influence at a diftance. We paffed the long chain until
we came to Fairfield, which compofes
that grand crefcent every perfon upon
Windermere looks up to with fuch re-
fpeĉt. In the rear of it is Flinty Grove,
in Deep-dale Head, where we look down
into the entrance of Patterdale, and
over the champaign part of Weftmoreland, including a large part of Cumberland.

Angle tarn, famous for fifh, cuts the
centre of the mountains before us, and,
though but fmall, is deferving of note.

The grove takes its name from fmall
flints, and appears as if it had never produced one blade of verdure, whilft its
neigh-

neighbour, St. Sunday Crag, is a bold
moſſy contraſt.

At one time we ſaw ſeven pieces of
water ; and, as the tide was coming in
on the Lancaſter ſands, we had many
ſalt-water lakes, which were terminated
by the weſtern ſea, an expanſe of blue,
far as the eye could reach, and throws
all the lakes in the world out of ſight ;
for, wherever the ocean is to be ſeen,
the eye imperceptibly reſts upon it ; and,
I dare ſay, if a man was in a contem-
plative mood, and had an opportunity
of looking at fine land proſpects on one
ſide, and the ſea on the other, he would
forſake ſubſtance for ſurface—with ſuch
intuition does the mind dwell upon an
expanſe of water, ſkirted by the ho-
rizon.

At a quarter paſt ſeven, after a tight
tug, we reached a mountain that would
make a fine race-courſe. We then
ſteeply deſcended to a tarn half a mile
below

below us, and had a bird's-eye view of
Grafsmere, at the fame time looking
over Helm Crag; which has a ferru-
ginous appearance, defcending towards
the tarn, which we judged to be an
amazing depth, from its very dark look.
This water is hid in three mountains,
headed by Seat Sandal. When we came
to it, I was with difficulty diffuaded
from drinking, I had fuch an ungovern-
able thirft upon me—I looked—and
longed—but conquered.

We then clambered to a heap of
ftones upon Grifdale Pike, or, as it is
called by the country people in remembrance of fome ruftic fun, " DOLLY
WAGGON PIKE ;" and I may venture to
fay fhe has a more commanding profpect
than any Dolly in the kingdom. To the
Weft, immenfe mountains, that hide the
vale of Borrowdale, fhewing three lakes
and the fea bounding them : to the Eaft,
fleecy clouds are rolling about the hills :
and fhe appears (from our fituation) the
head

head of a delightful valley, and of Ullfwater; plainly fhewing us Gowborough
Park, Dunmallart Head, and the outlet
of the lake.

We are in the midft of fharp whirlwinds, which ruftle up the dry mofs, and,
by lifting up the fkirts of my coat, have
given fome fine coolers to my back.
Thefe eddies are as refrefhing as a fea-
breeze in hot climates, and which is em-
phatically called " The Doctor."

On Whelp fide we fee Baffenthwaite
lake; and, after declining in order to
afcend the South-eaft flank of Helvellyn,
a hill, a mile long, extends to the eaftward; fo very narrow you might apparently fit acrofs any part of the ridge.
—The clouds are flying before the wind,
and reflect their fhadows fo fantaftically,
that beggars what we admired when upon
Windermere. But, as we have had a
hard march, I will clofe this chapter.

CHAP.

CHAP. XXII.

HELVELLYN.

Helvellyn Man—Differently named—Liberty taken by the Author out of Compliment to the Duke of Norfolk—A slight Sketch of his Character—Appearance of Ullswater Lake from Helvellyn—Descent to a Spring—Our extreme Joy—A Copy of Verses.

AT half past nine we reached Helvellyn Man, the highest point of this famous mountain. As many hills and particular parts of mountains have different names, according to the whim of separate villages, or the shapes they appear in to them, and as the summit of Helvellyn has several, I would not wish to
be

be thought officious, if I fhould call the higheft point Norfolk Point, in honour of the noble Duke, who has been upon it. You may not only overlook many hundred acres of his property, but you have a great command over a country through which his benevolence is unbounded.

It is not fo much from his exalted rank, as his familiar manners, that he has gained the ineftimable love of the people; he fpeaks to every one he meets, and he takes as much pleafure in ftooping into a cottage, as the proud man does at bowing into a palace. Make enquiry from the firft man, woman, or child, you meet in the North; and if your heart values the great in proportion as they are good, you will be proud of your noble countryman.

The view is growing more hazy; ftill the magnificence around us is beyond defcription; mountains towering above hills,

hills, as if they were parents of numerous families, and Helvellyn is the centre of them.

Skiddow is below us to the North. Crofs Fell is large enough to be vifible from an exalted fummit, and is only exceeded by Ingleborough in Yorkfhire, which holds her crowned head amidft a chain of hills, and feems from her height deferving of her royal appearance.

Old Man is juft in fight, and Old Friends ought not to be forgotten.— Place Fell cuts off a branch of Ullfwater, and makes the fhape of the lake refemble a pair of breeches ; inlaid with pafturage upon ground called the Old Church, becaufe there had probably been one there, and which is as rich as nature and induftry can make it.

Juft under is Red tarn, fhaped like a Bury pear : if I had but a draught of it, it would be worth all the fruit in the
world,

world, for my tongue cleaves to the roof
of my mouth.

Ravens are croaking ; and the wind,
which did not blow when I began to
write, is coming on in whiftling flurries.

We took a fweep to the right, and,
defcending about two hundred yards,
came to a charming fpring, with many
fheep about it, furrounded by a fmall
plot of the livelieft verdure, which muft
be a nibbling treafure to them ; we will
fuppofe they hold their *converzationes*
here, and they flew at our approach.

None but thofe who know the joy of
meeting a fpring when it is not expected,
can conceive my feelings when I found
myfelf feated on the wet grafs ; I would
inftantly have fwallowed a quantity, but
my friend, with the affiftance of pru-
dence, reminded me I had half a manchet
in my pocket, which I fteeped, and
feafted fomewhat in the fame manner
that

that Gil Blas and the ftrolling player
did, which adventure the facetious Le
Sage, with his accuftomed happinefs of
defcription, has handed down to us.
When I had ate my bread, I clofed my
mouth with the beverage, and faw,
whilft my head was fqueezed under the
herbage, how eagerly I enjoyed the
limpid draught.

The following verfes * were begun
upon Helvellyn, and fince finifhed in remembrance of the refrefhment received
from the fpring, vifited Auguft 2, 1792.
The reader will be difappointed if he
expects any of the fine-fpun thoughts of
fafhionable poetry. They are plain verfes,
that will tell you the progrefs of our laborious walk, and they may perhaps fatigue you ; but recollect, they may not
infringe upon poetical propriety if they
do, for they are upon a fatiguing fubject.

* See the Gentleman's Magazine for November, 1792.

M   I. THE

I.

THE full-orb'd moon o'er Loughrig * Fell,
Ting'd the rough crag with golden fpell
　　At the approach of morn ;
No clouds the lofty cliffs o'erhung,
No breath of wind refreſhing ſung
　　Through the upſtanding corn.

II.

O'er mountains high, to valleys deep,
And higher ſtill, and ſtill more ſteep,
　　We bruſh'd the early dew.
Toil wet the brow; the beauties round
Leſſen'd the labour of the ground,
　　And ſpurr'd us to purſue.

III.

Ranging the eye with full delight,
A ſheet of water cheer'd the ſight,
　　Entomb'd in mountains drear.
My Mentor urg'd me to go on—
" Leave, leave the tempting draught alone,
　　" For danger lurketh there.

* The head of Ambleſide valley from the Salutation
inn.

IV. Again

IV.

Again we toil'd—a fteep afcent *
Made me with parched tongue repent
    I had not dar'd to try.
The choice was paft—yet through the toil
The eye was pleafur'd all the while,
    And cover'd many a figh.

V.

Ye Naiads of the brooks fo gay,
That on the cryftal furface play,
    Invifible to all ;
Should you retire beneath the deep,
May you in peaceful caverns fleep,
    Lull'd by the cataract's fall.

VI.

Or, if on airy wing you fly,
Attend the cleaving, thirfty figh,
    To mountains bend your way ;
Exert your powers, and from below
Enforce fome hidden fount to flow,
    T' affuage the heat of day.

* Grifdale Pike.
VII. Helvellyn's

VII.

Helvellyn's height at laft we gain'd,
And, panting for relief, remain'd
    To mark th' extenfion round;
Then down with lighter pace we bent;
A spring l—the cleareft Heav'n e'er fent—
    I kifs'd the moiften'd ground.

VIII.

Eager I drew the cooling ftream,
And all fatigue was gone—a dream!
    Helvellyn's praife to fing;
Thy carpet was the livelieft green,
Thy fheep the fwifteft I have feen,
    All owing to thy fpring.

IX.

Thy profpects are beyond compare;
Mountains, and dales, and hills appear,
    And Ocean bounds the whole;
Thy bubbling was the fweeteft found
That ever tinkled o'er the ground
    To lull th' enraptur'd foul.

X. Neareft

X.

Neareſt to Heaven * !—unrivall'd flow ;
May torrents ne'er deface thy brow,
    No ſeaſon dry thy courſe !
May all thy ſheep untroubled live,
And man the limpid draught receive
    At thy enliv'ning ſource !
Then ſhall bold man Helvellyn's views make known ;
Refreſh'd by thee—on Skiddow's height look down.

    * I believe, the higheſt ſpring in England.

M 3   CHAP.

CHAP. XXIII.

HELVELLYN.

Vanity on overlooking six Mountains—Mossy Sheathing giving way—Rolling Stones down Helvellyn—Caution in the Descent —Wyburn Lake—A Sheep-Birth—A grand Canopy—A hearty Breakfast— And a chatty old Woman.

THE six magnificent mountains, we looked up to with such admiration when we went to Patterdale, were under Helvellyn; and the idea struck me that I was their superior.

Great part of the mossy sheathing is either washed away by torrents of rain, or disrobed by whirlwinds, perhaps by both; and I should not wonder if it would

would foon be bare, for, when a rent is once made, it muft give way.

On a part near the fummit, where there has (I think) been a watch-tower, we tried the experiment of rolling ftones down a precipice. Many have been delighted in tumbling them down young hills; they may therefore imagine a large ftone bouncing off with a great bow, then dafhing from fide to fide of indented ragged chafms, until it jumped upon a heap of ftones, or hopped diftantly into the valley.

After our luxurious banquet, we defcended progreffively, until we came to another range, which was fteep and unpleafant, being covered with loofe ftones we could not truft to. We then came to that rife which is only feen from the high road, and which is often fuppofed the top of the mountain. Here we opened upon the peaceful view of Wyburn, beautiful though unadorned with

M 4   trees;

trees; its crooked-fided lake, from the darknefs of its colour, muft be very deep. I took an opportunity of refting upon a fnug fheep-birth, that was almoft an afylum to me, for we were obliged to traverfe with the utmoft caution, the ground was fo hard and fteep; and, although I was mafter of my refolution, as I had only one arm to depend upon, the hand of which was wearily bliftered; I would not, whilft defcending, have looked at any thing but my feet, for all the pro-fpects in the univerfe *.

* Partridge, who acts as guide, as boots, poftilion, and boatman, at the Salutation Inn, might have brought us down an eafier defcent; but, as he had been out with a chaife all night, he was perhaps induced, from fatigue, to take us the neareft way. We never refted five minutes, that he did not fall afleep, and gave us a little nafal mufic, and which hindered me noting fo fully as I wifhed to have done. I think it proper to give this caution, that future ramblers may make choice of which road they pleafe. As to honeft Partridge, he meant no wrong, for he is fo bold a mountaineer, he can go any where that a fheep could, and, I dare fay, thinks every perfon can do the fame.

How-

However, between ten and eleven we found ourfelves in the high road, and tript lightly to the Cherry-tree. I have always remarked, after defcending a fteep mountain, I feel lighter and walk brifker than my ufual beft pace. We were to the weftward of the opening of Seat Sandal, a canopy I have mentioned more than once before, particularly in the grand rain fcene, when on Helm Crag; and which muft always be deferving of remembrance, as I now leave it, perhaps, for the laft time.

The public-houfe is half way between Amblefide and Kefwick, and they gave us a breakfaft fit for labouring men. We had mutton ham, eggs, butter-milk, whey, tea, bread and butter, and they afked us if we chofe to have any cheefe, all for feven-pence apiece. Do not imagine, good reader, that we glutto-nized; we did not forget our repaft upon Helvellyn—however, we did our duty at this fecond breakfaft.

Two

Two grandmothers were in the kitch-
en; one was employed in nurſing, the
other in toaſting bread, and the landlady in ſpreading out the table. One of
the old women was between eighty and
ninety, and ſaid ſhe had ſeen ſixteen
landlords out in a houſe that wiſhed to
oppoſe them. She was a chatty old lady,
and, as both my friend and I wiſhed to
give free ſcope to every one we ſpoke to,
ſhe had the clack of her ſex, and the
privilege of years to ſay what ſhe pleaſed;
ſhe performed both parts of queſtions
and anſwers, and told us ſhe had
been a pretty ſhepherdeſs in her time,
and that ſhe had been too often upon
Skiddow in her youth to be ill in her old
age.

I mention theſe to make known how
healthful and cheery they live under the
Cherry-tree. I think a chatty old woman,
when ſhe is not too much upon the diffu-
ſive,

five, is a moft cheerful companion, and ought to command a refpectful hearing.

We concluded this morning walk was very near thirty miles along a range of hills; for, although we rofe up fome of them flow, we could not help fometimes defcending very faft. From the point where we began to mount Rydal Hill, to the part of the road where we defcended, was nine miles upon a level; and we had above a mile to return to the Cherry-tree, which lengthened our time to above feven hours.

CHAP.

CHAP. XXIV.

KESWICK.

*Road to Kefwick—Kefwick Fair—Once fa-
mous for Leather—Reafons for its Decay
—Mirth replaces Profit.*

THE road along Wyburn Lake is pleafant.   There are three neat bridges over
fmall grafs-plot iflands, which were fet off
to advantage from a groupe of cattle grazing upon them, and fpreading in the ebb
water around.   The overhanging rocks
are often grand, and the road being good
we fpanked along.   Two miles farther
we faw the head of a waterfall flowing
from Legerthwaite tarn ; it was buried
about one hundred yards in a chafm its
former force had occafioned, came out
with the force of water from a fteam-en-
gine,

gine, and we then loft it again. We once faw it from the irregularity of the rock in five feparations.   There was a fhady hill on the oppofite fide of the road, whofe dark brow looked refrefhed from the life the waterfall gave the fcene.

This road is well variegated, and we ftopped two miles from Kefwick to take a kind of leave of Helvellyn, though we knew we were to fee it again.   At the fame time we had a fight of Skiddow. Thefe mountains, towering over all around them, feemed to challenge each other for pre-eminence ; and the decifion might be on either fide, if we were to judge from the eye only.

The hedges, as you approach the town, are fingularly pretty, and the woodbine was charmingly entwined. The vale of Kefwick is rich, but too broad and extenfive for landfcape.   As we approached the town, it looked neat ; and the church, which is feparated from it,

is

is a handfome double-roofed one. When we entered, it was their annual fair; there were but few booths, and thofe moftly for gew-gaws. It was once a confiderable market for leather, and within thefe ten years there ufed to be ten or a dozen waggon-loads of that ftaple; but a market has been eftablifhed at Settle in Yorkfhire, that has deftroyed their trade, and there is not this day one fkin to be fold. However, there is a difpofition to recollect it, and it will probably be always a red-letter day, for a fiddle is twanging in every ale-houfe, and they feem determined to make up in mirth what is wanting in profit.

CHAP.

CHAP. XXV.

Crofsthwaite's Mufeum—Refinement in lit-
tle Vagrants—Defcription of the Play-
Houfe—Their Mufic—A full Houfe—
Reafons for leaving it—Awoke by Dan-
cing—A blind Fidler.

WE went in the afternoon to fee Crofs-
thwaite's Mufeum, and entered to the
mufic of one of his new-invented Æolian
harps. He fhewed us feveral other fpecimens of his mechanical talents, and
perhaps he poffeffes fome valuable curi-
ofities. We were fo pleafed with his apparent *naïveté* of manners and defire to
oblige, we purchafed his plan of the
lakes, and found it ufeful. I would recommend ftrangers to drop a fhilling,
at leaft, at the Mufeum. In rainy weather

ther it muſt be a good morning's lounge.
As to the little quarrels amongſt the VIR-
TUOSOS of the town, travellers ſhould
pay no attention to them, but encourage
merit wherever they find it; for, in little ſtates as well as in great ones, "Doc-
tors will diſagree."

When you leave the Muſeum, a hand-
organ ſtrikes up, and he never ſees any
of his cuſtomers paſs the houſe without
a tune of acknowledgement; I think we
got about ſix. You will eaſily find out
where he lives; for, in his hand-bills,
he ſays it is "the largeſt houſe in town,"
and he has glaſſes in every direction to
ſhew him people paſſing in the ſtreet.

We afterwards walked to the head of
the lake, to judge what we had in future
to expect. Some children troubled us
by aſking for money, and uſeleſsly running before us to open a gate. We gave
one of the boys a penny, and becauſe one
halfpenny was a bad one, he aſked us
to

to change it. This refinement of beg-
gary in the young vagrant hindered us
from countenancing them; and they
ceafed to trouble us.

In the evening we went to fee the Merchant of Venice in an unroofed houfe.
The fky was vifible through niches of
boards laid acrofs the upper beams. The
walls were decorated, or rather hid, with
caft-off fcenes, which fhewed in many
places a rough unplaftered wall.

Some of the actors performed very
well, and fome very middling. Their poverty fhall ftop the pen of criticifm; and
their endeavours were well expreffed by
their motto—" TO PLEASE."

Between the acts, a boy, feated upon
an old rufh chair in one corner of the
ftage, ftruck up a fcrape of a fiddle. By
his drefs, which was once a livery, we
fuppofe he was a fervant of all work,
and had belonged to the manager in bet-
N   ter

ter days. But I muſt do Shylock the
juſtice to ſay, he performed well; and
although no perſon bawled out " this is
" the Jew that Shakſpeare drew," when
he was expreſſing his ſatiſfaction at Antonio's misfortunes, a little girl in the gallery roared, " O MAMMY! MAMMY! what
" a ſad wicked fellar that man is!"

The houſe was as full as it could poſſibly cram, and my friend counted but
thirty-ſix ſhillings' worth of ſpectators
in the pit, at eighteen pence a head, including a young child that ſqualed a
ſecond to the Crowdero of the houſe.
Perhaps, as the actors were ſo near the
audience, it was frightened by Shylock's
terrific look. Whilſt I remained, not even
the " Huſh a be babby" of its mother
had any effect.

I found it ſo extremely hot, and I felt
ſome knees preſs ſo hard upon my back,
againſt a piece of curtain which com-

2   poſed

pofed the feparation of pit and gallery, that I took my departure, and enjoyed a walk to the head of Derwenter lake. The moon was in fplendour, and had juft efcaped out of a cloud that had really a terrific look. Skiddow and the hills to the right were buried in blacknefs, and there was an eafterly breeze which feem-ed to affift the moon in getting the bet-ter of her fable enemies.

It was a fight that well repaid me for having left the play-houfe, and fent me to bed in full thought of ferioufnefs : but I was foon awoke by the found of a fiddle from the next alehoufe, and by moft vi-olent dancing to it. I threw up my win-dow, with a determination to be pleafed at what kept me awake. Applaufe and laughter attended every dancer. The in-ftrument was continually going ; but, with all my endeavours, I could only make out one tune ; and, although I never heard any thing like it before, it is ftill buzzing in my head. As to mufic,

N 2   what

what fignified mufic! Such dancing as theirs wanted but little to induce the heel and toe to beat time to each other; and they were determined to wear leather, if they could not fell it.

Whilft I am writing, a blind fidler is reeling by the inn, and, as well as I can make out, is playing Lady Coventry's minuet, with his own variations.

CHAP.

CHAP. XXVI.

DERWENTER LAKE.

*Went upon the Lake—A Bottom Wind—Ef-
fect on the Boat—Floating Ifland—Silver
Hill—Beautiful Compafs of the Lake—
Its Clearnefs—Lowdore Water-Fall—
Wild Fruit—Curly-headed Children.*

WE had Hutton's boat, and failed
round Pocklington's ifland, which is decorated with St. Mary's church, built as
an object; a boat-houfe in imitation of
a Weftmoreland chapel; a fort, and a
decent porter's lodge.

The houfe feems more calculated for
viewing the various profpects around it,
than for fetting them off: and it would
appear to greater advantage if it were

N 3   white-

white-wafhed ; but it is now feldom inhabited, and the novelty of a regatta is
evaporated.   At Portinfcale there is another houfe belonging to the fame owner,
pleafantly fituated ; but the wings have
fuch a moufe-trap look, it is a disfigured
object.

The wind was foutherly, and, although
very moderate, the lake was violently agitated by what is called *a bottom wind*,
which occafioned fuch confufion upon
the furface, we were obliged to keep
clofe in land ; fo very near, one of the
oars often touched ground ; in many
places it was poppling, as I have feen
when a ftrong current oppofes a ftrong
wind ; and in others the waves were high,
and covered with breakers.   The guide
was afraid to venture on the middle of
the lake, as he faid it would be dangerous.   This I could hardly think ; but
it might have been laborious, as we had
only two oars to row and fteer an un-
wieldy

wieldy boat, and we might have got a ducking from the fpray.

It is faid, Kefwick Lake often wears this appearance a day or two previous to a ftorm; and, when violently agitated at the bottom, an ifland arifes, and remains upon the furface fome time; on the laft emerging, it was fplit in the middle, and the guide failed through it. The grafs and the mofs are as green as a meadow, which foon unite and become confiftent: there are very few people in the neighbourhood who have not been upon it.

We paffed all the iflands, and opened upon a retired bay, which prefented us with Silver Hill, a houfe built in the cottage ftyle, and, from not attempting at finery, has an interefting appearance; but I think it would look more in character if it was roofed with thatch inftead of blue flate.—The owner of it, who is one of your great farmers, has

N 4   made

made a road along the fide of the mountain, leading from Kefwick to Buttermere, hoping to induce the country people to prefer it to a lower one they have
been accuftomed to ; but they are either
afraid of being blown into the lake in
rough weather, or are fo fond of the old
path, they are returned to it again, and
the new one is a defacement to the hill.

Nearly oppofite to Silver Hill is Barrow Cafcade hall, a third uninhabited
houfe, belonging to the owner of the
ifland, a perfon who farms a good deal.
This gentleman's land may be known by
handfome gates, and the initials of his
name in wood, that reach from the top
to the bottom of them. The fummer-
houfe, and a waterfall, fhewing its foam
through the trees, have a pleafing effect ; the houfe, too, would look well if
the wings were raifed, or if it was without them, and if there was a door in
front.

Here

Here it is one mile and a half acrofs, and comprehends an almoft circular piece of water, which, as a lake, far furpaffes Windermere.

We made a crefcent to the outlet, and found it margined by thick reeds, and the cleareft water I ever faw, fhewing at a great depth its green bottom. We landed near a public-houfe, and walked up to a ruinous mill at the foot of Lowdore waterfall. It muft be a tremendous cataract after rain; but the weather has been fo long fair, we were only left to judge from the rugged ftones which reach to the fummit, and which muft have been left by torrents. It looks as if the afcent was difficult; but I am told it is not. Two perpendicular rocks are centinels, and though the one to the right appears as tall as the oppofite, we are deceived from fituation, for it is not half the height.

As

As you defcend from thefe rocks, ftep afide, and you may find, as we did, the largeft wild ftrawberrries I ever eat, and innumerable rafpberries. After a delicious tafte, we met three children hand in hand, with heads as rough as curls could make them. I gave each of them a half-penny; and, without being able to diftinguifh whether they were boys or girls, they threw their little poles at me.

Dr. Dalton, in an elegant poem addreffed to two young ladies at Whitehaven, fpeaking of the rocks of Lodore, has the following beautiful reflections:

" Horrors like thefe at firft alarm,
But foon with favage grandeur charm,
And raife to nobleft thought the mind;
Thus nigh thy fall, Lodore, reclin'd;
The craggy cliff, impending wood,
Whofe fhadows mix o'er half the flood;
The gloomy clouds, with folemn fail,
Scarce lifted by the languid gale
O'er the capp'd hill, and darken'd vale;

The

The rav'ning kite, and bird of Jove,
Which round th' aërial ocean rove,
And, floating on the billowy sky,
With full expanded pinions fly,
Their fluttering or their bleating prey,
Thence with death-dooming eye survey;
Channels by rocky torrents torn,
Rocks to the Lake in thunder borne,
Or such as o'er our heads appear
Suspended in their mid career,
To start again at his command,
Who rules fire, water, air, and land;
I view with wonder and delight,
A pleasing, tho' an awful sight.
For, seen with them, their verdant isles
Soften with more delicious smiles,
More tempting twine their empty bowers,
More lively glow their purple flowers;
More smoothly slopes the border gay,
In fairer circle bends the bay.
And last, to fix our wand'ring eyes,
Thy roofs, O Keswick, brighter rise,
The lake and lofty hills between,
Where giant Skidaw shuts the scene."

Amongst other particulars, he laments
the violations of those sacred woods and
groves, by the Commissioners of Greenwich

wich Hofpital ordering the woods to be
cut down, which had for ages fhaded the
margin and promontories of that lovely
lake—For,

" Where the rude ax with heaved ftroke
Was never heard the nymphs to daunt,
Or fright them from their hallow'd haunt,"

There is, alas ! now,—

" The lonely mountain o'er,
And the refounding fhore,
A voice of weeping heard and loud lament ;
From haunted fpring and dale,
Edg'd with poplar pale,
The parting Genius is with fighing fent :
With flower-in woven treffes torn,
The nymphs in twilight fhade of tangled thickets
        mourn."

CHAP.

CHAP. XXVII.

DERWENTER LAKE.

Bowdore Stone—and many others forced from their Parent—Scope for Botany—Barrowdale—Afcend Caftle Crag—Interior Richnefs of Barrowdale—Wad Mine—Herbert's Ifland—A Reflection on it—The Lady Derwentwater's Efcape—Manager's Speech on having a thin Houfe.—A fhort Account of him.

WE proceeded into the entrance of Barrowdale, and came near the unadorned, but picturefque, village of Grange. Huge and mis-fhapen rocks were overhanging the road; on the breaking up of a froft, points of them are accuftomed to give way, and we faw many

3   fmooth

fmooth places whence they were forced.
Roots of old oak, hard as the rock, and
in fome parts feemingly engrafted in it,
had a ftriking effect ; and the whole was
a grand affemblage of the fublime.

One piece, named BOWDORE STONE,
which juft fkirts the road, demands being fpoken of, and one fhould think
would have required an earthquake to
have removed it *.   It is many hundred
thoufand tons weight, and has fallen in
fo nice a manner, it feems in equili-
brium : a fmall oak and afh grow in little niches where you cannot fee any foil.
The time of feparation from its parent
rock is unknown. Hutton has remembered it twenty years, and does not think
the trees grown.   A fhepherd has built

* Bowdore Stone is nineteen yards and a half in
length, and nine feet and a half in heighth ; it is by no
means one entire ftone, but a confolidated mafs, forced
by fome fhock from its native bed ; but at what period
no authentic account can be obtained.

a loofe

a loofe wall on both fides to fold his
fheep, or I am told it would refemble
the keel of a large fhip.

Two hundred yards before we came to
Bowdore Stone we faw an old crooked
hawthorn grow out of an old crooked
oak; and, at fome diftance beyond it, an
afh out of a holly. I mention thefe
engraftments becaufe I believe they are
occafioned either by the wind, or by
birds conveying berries, and are not the
ftudied experiment of man *.

Thofe who have a tafte for botany
muft be well repaid by fcrutinizing the
mofs and plants with which this neigh-

* This is by no means unfrequent in the North, efpecially in the vicinity of rooks and daws, which drop
feeds of various fhrubs into apertures or interftices of a
tree, and which are nourifhed by decayed leaves, and
moifture dropping from the parent; they flourifh with
apparent vigour for a time, but when the fcanty foil becomes infufficient for their maturer growth they wither
and decay.

bourhood

bourhood abounds; they may wander away a few hours with pleafure, and collect many things worth inveftigating and preferving.

As we advanced farther into Barrowdale we faw feveral of the quarry-men taking advantage of the dinner hour to wafh themfelves in the brook. We mounted Caftle Crag up a fteep zig-zag of loofe pieces of blue flate, until we came within a hundred and fifty yards of the top, which gave a good view of the vale and its mountains; Eagle Crag*, Bull mountain†, and others equally ragged. Upon reviewing the lake, the agitation, which was fo violent as we have noticed, had ceafed. We faw the ifland; the houfe fkirted our right, Crofthwaite church on

* From the eagle frequently building upon it.

† The perfon who farms the land, which includes this mountain, is obliged to keep a bull for the ufe of the valley; the echo is fo loud he makes himfelf mad very foon; and I believe it is now compromifed.

the

the left; and while we were admiring them the fun darted out, and fhewed the whole in fuch fair character, Kef- wick and its vales were plainly feen, and Skiddow for the firft time appeared a back-ground diftance. Not expecting this grand luminary, it was a moft en- chanting furprize.

Curiofity ought to have led us to the fummit, for it was once a Roman fta- tion; but we are told a trace of it is fcarcely difcernible. There have been many flate quarries upon the crag, which have entirely obliterated the appearance of ancient fortifications; for, the miners are not inclined to pay much attention to them, if there are any ftones that can be otherwife ufeful.

After feafting over the natural beauties around us, we entered farther into Bar- rowdale *; where the mountains form a
grand

* In the year 1745, all the farmers from a great diftance drove their cattle into this retired valley, as a

grand amphitheatre, yet neither fo magnificent or pleafing as the one around our
chafte favourite, Graffmere lake. Thefe
mountains have been, and we will ftill
hope are, rich in internal wealth.

The houfehold inhabitants farm their
own eftates, and the working-men moftly
get their bread in lead mines or in flate
quarries. At this place there is the only
wad mine * in the kingdom as yet dif-
covered, which has been occafionally worked and clofed fince the days
of queen Elizabeth : now they are afraid
the mine is exhaufted, and they are after
a retrieving fearch. In days of its fplendour, as much as was wanted for general
confumption was foon procured, and

fafety againft the rebel forces ; which was a noble
fupply for their favourite Duke. The days of incurfions
are imprinted on the minds of the people about the Lakes ;
and the rebel army entered into a part of England where
they had the moft rooted enemies.

* Black lead.

3   it

it was then clofed for a time ; however, they have a large ftock in referve.

The guide told us, he heard one of the workmen affirm he could get the value of one thoufand pounds worth in half an hour * ; when it is known how eafily it is procured, and how valuable a fingle pound weight is, it is to be credited.

* Mines, producing a ' fimilar kind of metal, have been found both in Germany and Scotland; but the qua-lity is very inferior, and the quantity procured from their richeft veins is inconfiderable when compared to this. I had an opportunity of feeing this fully illuftrated in the year 1781. An action was brought againft a perfon at Kefwick, for furreptitioufly obtaining wad from this mine, and configning it to an agent in London. The plea. fet up by the defendant was, that other mines of the fame kind were worked in Scotland, &c. The profecu-tor exhibited in court feveral fpecimens, which, upon infpection by fcientific people, were found to differ ma-terially in excellence from that of Kefwick ; and no one piece larger than an hen's egg, it was alleged, had ever been got in Germany or Scotland. Verdict for the plaintiff.

We

We returned to our boat, and made a direct line to Hubert's ifland, fo called after a religious hermit; the crumbled remains of his habitation are ftill feen ; and I even think for a worldly-minded man it would be no bad occafional retreat. We walked through a long avenue of fir trees (take care not to tumble, the fallen fir is fo flippery), and planted ourfelves under the fhade of fome large hollies, where we enjoyed a cool retreat, and as hearty a dinner as if we had been lords of the wad-mine.

I afterwards traverfed the ifland. The trees are various, high, and open ; and I returned with a blade of grafs meafuring fix and a half feet. I then landed upon Derwent ifland, the once fumptuous refidence of the unfortunate earl. There are many ftately trees, and I noticed very tall fycamores growing out of the bottom of hollies that had fallen to the faw.

You

You may trace the walls of the houfe ; but the materials were ufed to build Kef- wick Town-hall, and the inn in which I am writing. A farm-houfe is built on the oppofite fhore, where the ftables once ftood ; and that fide of the lake is for- feited to Greenwich Hofpital.

I could not help giving way to a cer- tain gloom of confideration. I was the only perfon upon the ifland ; a place once gladdened with the found of wealth and hofpitality : but, by a mifguided and ill-judged caufe, one of the fineft pro- perties in the kingdom was confifcated : innumerable nettles have fprung up where the manfion once ftood—vagrant emblems of diffolved property ; for, all its once-boafted grandeur is no more !

The earl of Derwentwater was much beloved, and he is handed down to the prefent people with refpect. They had

O 3

fo ftrongly the idea his lady perfuaded him to take the caufe he did, fhe became the hatred of the country, and, to avoid the effects of it, fhe one evening made her efcape over Walloh Crag, a very fteep afcent covered with loofe ftones. It was certainly a bold attempt; but, what is an undaunted woman incapable of undertaking, when her mind is afloat with either love or hatred!

We had not far to go to the pier, which clofed a very pleafant excurfion. My friend went to the play; but, as there were no more than four people in the houfe, the poor itinerants were obliged to return the money, which the manager did with a dafh of humour that did his acting great credit; for it could not come from the heart. " Gentlemen, be- " fore I return you your money, I will firft " fhew you our *elegant* Theatre." The fcene was drawn up—and the fcene was clofed—and fo, good night to you.

I had

I had remembered the manager when he was in much better plight, and have often heard general laughter at a ſtroke of humour he introduced in the character of Serjeant Kite, which is not in the play. Reading the articles of war to the affrighted clowns, he added, " Whatfo-" ever officer or ſoldier ſhall be found " guilty of building a church out of his " pay, ſhall ſuffer death, or ſuch other " puniſhment as ſhall be inflicted upon " him by the ſentence of a court mar-" tial."

As I was at that time recruiting, and out of remembrance to former days, I ſent for him, and purchaſed ſome tickets. His faded garb was thread-bare, and two pins in a certain part of his *inexpreſſibles* ſupplied the place of buttons. I aſked him ſome leading queſtions, that made him ſpeak about me ; but I found he was rather entering too fully into my follies ; and, as I did not think it fair to expoſe

O 4   myſelf

myfelf too much before my friend, I turned the converfation. In regard to the manager, I knew I was fafe. Fifteen years abfence has concealed my former features under the bulk that has gathered around them.

When we left Kefwick, I returned him the tickets under my name; and I dare fay he would be much furprized to find who it was that had purchafed them.

CHAP.

CHAP. XXVIII.

BUTTERMERE.

*Enchanting Walk—Newland Valley—Ruf-
tic Civility—Two Waterfalls—Mountain
Paftures—The Village of Buttermere.*

WE intended ftarting between two and
three, in hopes of feeing the fetting moon,
and the rifing fun upon Skiddow. We
were not fo fortunate, for it rained and
blew hard all night, and it was fine when
we went to bed : thus far the lake yefterday foreboded right. I was fo vexed
at this difappointment, I was defervedly
punifhed by being kept awake. However, the morning is clear, and we are
going to fet off to Buttermere.

We

We paffed along the Cockermouth road for a mile and a half; then turned towards Newland valley, keeping a moft enchanting fight of Baffenthwaite Lake, and frequently of Derwentwater, Kef-wick appearing to the beft advantage it can be feen in. Inftead of keeping the road, we dropt down fome fine paftures, until we came to a deep brook. The bridge had been carried away, a victim to the floods, which obliged us to go higher than the point we intended making; however, we found a ladder fome good-natured farmer had laid acrofs for general accommodation.

Before we reached the brook, we faw a treble-trunked oak ; the centre trunk was hollow, and a mountain-afh grew out of it ; about two yards down it, we broke a hole with our fticks, and the afh was ftrong and healthy.

We

We now reached the fide of the hill; and, being at a lofs which way to proceed, an old woman upwards of ninety, who was keeping houfe whilft the family were at harveft, directed us to the head of Newland, where we ftopped at a large farm-houfe, and afked, for fome whey. They had two machines at work (each of which could churn thirty pounds), and were making butter for falting. In an inftant we had two bowls of whey, and half a dozen hands offered us chairs. We were pleafed in thinking every trifle interefting that fo agreeably proves the active civility of thefe mountaineers: and who would not?

We had an eafy afcent to the head of Newland (a chaife could go up it) ,where there are two waterfalls upon one face of a mountain; the largeft is a very fine one, and, I fhould think, at any time equal to Lowdore, except in the terrific. It has now much the advantage; the

hills

hills around are covered with fheep and cattle ; and, as you return your eye upon the rich vale, you may fee Saddle Back, and look down upon the top of Caftle Crag : you then pafs a *defilé*, and, after a regular defcent of two miles, come fuddenly upon Buttermere chapel, with a fight of its ftraggled village, and Crummack lake. The head mountain and two fide ones are the moft beautiful carpets I ever faw, particularly the one to the right, which is covered with innumerable fheep ; and, although above two miles in length, and of a confiderable circumference, it is not defaced by one ftone.

CHAP.

CHAP. XXIX.

BUTTERMERE.

A Guide—Disagreeable Walk—Buttermere and Crummack Lakes—Sound of Scale-Force Waterfall—Its delicate Effect—Description of it—Reasons why the Inhabitants do not know the Names of their Mountains—Natural Child—Candour of his Mother—Manner of supporting their Poor —Chapel and School both one—Without a Clergyman—Inhabitants used to chuse their own—Schoolmaster officiates as Parson—Their Regret at the want of one.

AFTER ordering some dinner at a small ale-house, we got a son of Crispin to attend us to the cascade. The road we took was very uneven and boggy, with a num-

I

a number of beau-traps *. As we afcended, we gained a full view of both
Buttermere and.Crummock lakes, feparated by good land and a deep river.
There are two fmall iflands upon the
latter, and at the bottom the country
looks fertile; it is about two miles to
the waterfall, and we found it an uncomfortable tafk. But mountain-trou-
bles vanifh the inftant you behold the
object of a walk.

My ears firft caught the mellow found,
and, after clambering over a rough wall,
we came fuddenly upon the caufe of it.
I was loft in admiration ; in one of thofe
vacant delights, in which the mind
thinks of nothing but what is before it,
and makes you feel yourfelf more than
man ; I required a tap over the fhoulder
to return to mortality. I received it, and
I thus feebly defcribe the caufe of it.

* Stones in marfhy or foft ground, which, by heed-
lefsly ftepping on one fide of them, throw water over
the ftockings.

Scale-

Scale-Force waterfall is two hundred feet perpendicular, except where it flushes over a small jut. The steep on both sides is covered with variety of mofs, fern, afh, and oak, all fed by the conftant fpray, and flourifh in indefcribable verdure. The delicacy of the effect is heightened by being in a narrow chafm, a hundred yards in the rock, before it rufhes into the lower fall, at the point of which you have the grand view. Clamber up the left fide, and look into the firft bafin, and, although you may be wet with the fpray, you cannot help feeling the folemnity of this deep, this mufical abyfs, enchanting as verdure and melody can make it.

There has been no rain for nine days; yet it far exceeds any thing of the kind I ever faw, and the boafted one at Coo * in Germany finks below comparifon.

I fup-

* I once had the curiofity to ride over a moft dreadful way to fee this Waterfall. We were no fooner there but

I fuppofe we faw it in the beft ftate it
could be perceived in ; had it been after
rain,

but men and women began by throwing dogs above the
head of the fall. Our party were fo difgufted with it,
we paid them to defift. Many of the poor creatures were
lame : fometimes they are lucky enough to hit againft
a piece of rock, and are dafhed to death. Thofe that
furvive, fteal away as if they felt they were victims to
the unfeeling boors. The king of Sweden was there the
year before ; and they were furprized we could not be
pleafed with this cruel paftime, becaufe *he* was ; and,
though unfortunate in his death, and a hero through
life, of allowed humanity. I can never forget the ftory
of a poor cow, the *humane* boors forced down this waterfall, for his diverfion ; the beaft had a leg broke, and
his majefty was fo pleafed with the novelty, it was carried round to the head of the fall again, and was fo
lucky to fpoil more fport—for—it was killed.

The chapel was about the fize of Buttermere chapel,
and the *Curé* told us he did not receive ten pounds a year.
But I obferved the inhabitants had a greedinefs for money, and a rudenefs of manners becaufe we could not fa-
tisfy them all ; which does not difgrace our Englifh mountaineers. And, although two out of four of the party
were an Englifh and an Irifh curate, to fhew the happy
pre-

rain, it might have filled us with afto-
nifhment; but what would have become
of the verdure of the fides? The foam
would have nearly covered them. As we
faw it, every part was in unifon with the
mufic it created; the mind compre-
hended it, and carried away one of the
moft inimitable fcenes that ever enriched
the fancy of man, or graced the pencil
of a Moore.

On afking the guide the names of different hills, he faid, " In this valley we
" call them fo and fo—but other guides
" have gi'en them *feck* * fine neames, we
" do naw recollect um; bu we mun naw
" contract um, as they thinken umfelves
" cleverer folks than we are."

prejudice of their education, when the *Curé* complained
of the poverty of his receipts, they gave with liberality,
and he received with the fubmiffion of a learned beggar
accuftomed (by infinuation) to afk.

* Such.

P   We

We met a rofy boy with a fatchel on his back; he was going to one of the houfeholders for a ftated time. The poor live among the farmers in propor- tion as they are affeffed, and they are al- ways treated like one of the family. The only pauper at prefent is this little alien; his mother knew her frailties too well, and was too honeft to fwear to a father; therefore the villagers have taken the boy amongft them, and are going to fend him to fchool.

They faid with concern, until a fort- night ago they have had no regular fchoolmafter thefe two years; in fhort, fince the period of chufing their clergy- man was taken from them.

The chapel and the fchool ferve for both purpofes, and I could almoft reach the roof with my head. The inhabitants, time out of mind, ufed to appoint their own clergyman, and he was generally
chofen

chofen with full confent ; perhaps it was
the very pooreft livelihood in the kingdom, even with the addition of Queen
Anne's bounty ; but it was a vehicle for
a minor prieft to get fuperior orders,
and there never was a want of candidates : they now fay they have loft their
right, at any rate they do not claim one ;
and, whatever may be the reafon, they
are left to go to Heaven as quietly as
they can *.

By the augmentation from Queen
Anne's bounty, it requires inftitution
as a vicarage by ftatute, and confe-
quently a refident minifter is indifpen-
fable." The fchoolmafter, without being a clergyman, officiates as fuch ;
and one from Lorton, the parifh-church,
comes about once in fix weeks to admi-
nifter the facrament, which may be the
means of preferving the bounty.

* As the chapel enjoys Queen Anne's bounty, fhould
not the Diocefan take care they have a proper paftor ?
but I cannot fuppofe he is informed of it.

In

In this forlorn manner is the fervice performed in the village of Buttermere. Luckily it could not have happened in a village where it appears lefs wanted ; but, as good harmlefs people always regret the lofs of a good cuftom, they regret it.

CHAP.

CHAP. XXX.

BUTTERMERE.

Number of Families—Their Riches—Mode of paying Ale Duty, and of providing Provisions—Of procuring Surgeons for the Sick—A Rainbow—Never but one Chaise in the Valley—Sally of Buttermere.

THE village consists of fourteen families, and some of them are rich people; that is, they may have fifty pounds a year landed property, and healthful flocks of sheep. We looked into a kitchen that Crispin said belonged to the richest man in the place; and I never saw furniture shine brighter in my life; to be sure, it was Saturday, and that is a polishing day in every cottage in the kingdom ; and many a time and oft, in the humble period of my varied life, have I been delighted to fee the Saturday polifh, under a thatch which feemed never to want it, and where my honoured and honeft friend has ftill the hufbandman who lived with his father forty years ago. His fuccefs might place him in what is called a modern good houfe, but his heart keeps him under the roof that was refpected by his father ; and, from the decency with which he brings up his fmiling family, I dare think the name of DITCHFIELD will always be the owner of it. 1 hope always to fee it fo, and would fooner vifit it than the fineft houfe of grandeur.

We had falt provifions and vegetables for dinner, and I do not think there was a frefh joint in the valley. The ale was home-brewed, and good, but rather too ftrong for our tafte. If you are fond of ftrong ale, I muft tell you, Buttermere is reckoned famous for it.

Wine

Wine and fpirits * are not fold here, and they are fo far from the excife, they pay their duty by compofition, tenpence halfpenny a week; the landlady fays they do not fometimes fell fix pennyworth a week; but, as her hufband is one of the head quarry-men, his companions often make amends, for " her ale is as " gud as ony in aw Chriftendum."

On our return, we met a woman with a loaded horfe; fhe had been to Kefwick market, laying-in meat and other neceffaries for herfelf and neighbours. This amicable cuftom is equalled by the following; when a perfon is fick, or a woman about to lie-in, a horfeman is fent to Kefwick or Cockermouth for a fur-

* A ftranger came to this ale-houfe, faid he was very ill, and afked for a glafs of fpirits. She told him, fhe had no licence to fell any; but, in compaffion to his fituation, gave him a glafs. He forced her to be paid for it; —then lodged an information againft her; and fhe was obliged to pay the FINE.

P 4   geon,

geon, and the neighbours fend a relay of horfes to expedite him.

We reached the *defilé* with a frefh breeze, but a hot fun. We were afraid we fhould have been much incommoded by lofing the former ; luckily the mountain that kept the breeze from us, likewife hid the fun ; fo we enjoyed a pleafant walk along a gentle defcent. I mention this for information to thofe who may walk or ride this road, as, after fix in the evening, it is under fhade until you come to Portinfcale.

When we came to the Cockermouth road, we had a rich fight of a rainbow extending from Kefwick, and juft including Lowdore fall. It was rendered more beautiful by a watery tinge on the tops of the hills, and by the fun's partially leaving them fhewing which was the higheft.

The

The landlady had never feen but one chaife in the valley, which came from Cockermouth, and left it at the Kefwick road; fhe fpoke of it as a phænomenon.

I have fince met with the party; it was an excurfion foon after marriage. They are too valuable to their numerous friends, amongft which number I have the happinefs to think myfelf, ever to run any more mountain rifks. They were not aware of the danger, and I believe this cured them.

SALLY OF BUTTERMERE.

Her mother and fhe were fpinning woollen yarn in the back kitchen. On our going into it, the girl flew away as fwift as a mountain fheep, and it was not until our return from Scale Force that we could fay we firft faw her. She brought in part of our dinner, and feemed to be about fifteen. Her hair was thick and long, of a dark brown, and, though unadorned

adorned with ringlets, did not feem to want them; her face was a fine oval, with full eyes, and lips as red as vermilion; her cheeks had more of the lily than the rofe; and although fhe had never been out of the village (and I hope will have no ambition to wifh it), fhe had a manner about her which feemed better calculated to fet off drefs, than drefs *her*. She was a very Lavinia,

> " Seeming, when unadorn'd, adorn'd the moft."

When we firft faw her at her diftaff, after fhe had got the better of her firft fears, fhe looked an angel; and I doubt not but fhe is the reigning lily of the valley.

Ye travellers of the Lakes, if you vifit this obfcure place, fuch you will find the fair SALLY OF BUTTERMERE.

CHAP.

CHAP. XXXI.

SKIDDOW.

Surmount Skiddow—Delightful Views—The Source of the River Caldew—Ifle of Man —Ireland—The Sun fetting in Scotland— Severe Cold—Dotterell.

WE arrived at half paft feven at the vicarage ; and from a horfe-ftone in the court-yard had a noble command of Derwentwater. Turn in at a gate, and both lakes are feen. Winding to the right, we have a complete fight of La-trigg, a mountain pafture, and we foon front moft of the mountains of Cumber-land, including Black Coomb in Lan-cafhire. We overlook the grange of Barrowdale, the vales of Newland and

St.

St. John's, and to the eaftward Burns
and Thilkirk.

As we proceed up Skiddow, we fee
a very fmall fpring, from which the
Caldew has its rife ; and, as it defcends,
we can notice its increafing breadth,
from the many ftragglers it takes in.
The Caldew runs with great velocity
through moft romantic valleys, until it
paffes by Carlifle ; it afterwards falls into
the Eden, a river that has previoufly received many others, and then nobly en-
ters the Irifh fea at Rocliffe.   When we
reach the top, we open the crown of Ingleborough, and the range of hills to the
champaign part of Northumberland ;
we have the Chiviot hills, and the great
chain to the point of Mull in Galloway.   The fun is fetting over Hawthorn
ifland, belonging to lord Selkirk, partially tinging both coafts. And I cannot
omit an opportunity of faying, it is a
glorious emblem of an Union that has
made two people one, and, by making

our interefts the fame, ftopped a tide of
Britifh blood, and turned our hatred into
affection. By carrying the eye to the
Mull of Galloway, we juft fee the North
of Ireland, and diftinctly the length of
the Ifle of Man.

The river Derwent runs by Cockermouth into the fea at Workington, both
which places are very vifible; as is St.
Bee's Head, above the harbour of Whitehaven, with upwards of twenty veffels
under fail.

Tarn Waddling, near Plumpton in
this county, and bordering upon Northumberland, from being folitary, looks
well even in the growing haze around it,
as every little variety tends to fet off the
great whole.

The fun is dropping over the Scottifh
hills, and at a quarter paft eight is juft
departed to enlighten other worlds; its
laft powers have made the writing red

as

as blood. Solway Frith, though an arm of the fea, appears like an immenfe lake, and the Heavens have fuch a variety of tints, vain muft be every attempt to depict them.

We were at the fartheft heap of ftones, covered from the Eaft wind, when I wrote the above. The air was thin and cool, but, when we took our departure, we were obliged to run over the hard furface as expeditioufly as we could, and, before we were under cover from the wind, drops (not poetical) ran down our cheeks, and, faving your prefence, uninvited from my nofe. My fingers were almoft benumbed; but, when we came under cover from the wind, we took time to breathe, and found the evening foft and fine.

We faw fome dotterels upon the fummit, that let us approach within eight yards; and, if I had not thrown a ftone at them, I dare fay we might have come

near

near enough to have thrown " falt on
" their tails." They fuck their food
from under the fmall ftones, under which
they build their nefts ; and, what is remarkable, have only frequented Skiddow
feven years. Thefe birds are fat and fweet
flavoured, have only three claws, a long
cylindrical bill, and are rather above the
fize of a thrufh, though coloured like
one, excepting a black ftreak upon the
head. It is with difficulty they can be
forced to leave Skiddow; and, when they
do, they never reft long upon other
mountains. Hutton has one in his re-
pofitory, the recollection of which gives
me an opportunity of defcribing it*.

* " The dotterel builds and incubates upon the higheft
mountains in this country, and early in the fpring defcends to the lower craggy hills, efpecially in the vicinity
of Orton and Afby, where many of them are fhot, as well
for their delicacy of tafte, as for their feathers, which
are in high eftimation with the anglers, for making ar-
tificial flies."

CHAP.

CHAP. XXXII.

Mountains—The old Man—Skiddow—Hel-
vellyn, and Helm Crag.

I Have obferved all the large mountains run from South-eaft to North-weft, and there are generally three ranges, inclu-ding the fummit ; leffer hills are as uncer-tain as the waves.

The profpects from the Old Man are extenfive, but not fo interefting as from Helvellyn or Skiddow : the afcent is te-dious, from being obliged to go the greateft part of the way by fhort uneven zigzags, made to convey flate from the quarries, and which tend to craze the head. I am told, when the weather is

clear

clear, you may count twenty lakes, and the fummit is not defaced by a ftone. The fpring will be found a pleafant confideration, and will help to leffen fatigue; but you will find yourfelf fo very hot, you muft drink with great caution; a gulp of brandy, or forcing yourfelf to eat, will leffen the danger; and, although I drank without feeling any hurt, it is too dangerous an experiment to recommend, and I think it my duty to advife the thirfty not to imitate me.

The hills to the South-weft of Skiddow looked grand, from variety of light and fhade. We were fo much above them, they refembled gigantic waves after a ftorm; and as we did not fee Ireland, the Frith of Solway, or the Ifle of Man, from any other mountain, they enhance the other beauties they can boaft of; nor does any of the lakes look fo well from an eminence as Derwentwater, it is fo charmingly indented. There is no

Q   fpring

spring upon Skiddow * ; but, as the afcent is eafy, it is not fo much wanted.
It has once had a mofly fheathing, which
has been long given to the whirlwinds.
The want of it may, perhaps, be the rea-

* The mountain of Skidaw is about eleven hundred
yards perpendicular from the level of Broadwater.   It is
biparted at the fummit, bearing fome refemblance to the
antient poetic Parnaffus; and, with a kind of majeftic
emulation, beholds Scruffel Hill before it in Annandale
in Scotland.   By thefe two mountains, according as the
mifty clouds afcend or fall, the neighbouring fhepherds
make their prognoftication of the change of the weather,
which probably gave rife to the following diftich :

   If Skidaw hath a cap,
   Scruffel wots full well of that.

  There is alfo another faying, very commonly ufed in
thefe parts, concerning the height of this hill with two
others in this kingdom :

   Skidaw, Lauvellin, and Cafticand,
   Are the higheft hills in all England.

  Upon the top of this mountain there is a blue flate
ftone, about five feet and a half high, which they call
Skidaw Man.

fon of dotterels frequenting it, and may fix a preiod for the fpeculatift to imagine when it was left bare.

The approach to Helvellyn along the Rydal hills gives a multiplicity of land-fcapes, fhewing the fame mountains in various fhapes. The defcent is difficult, incommoded by loofe ftones, fmall rocks, or dry hard ground; I was obliged to prefs fo hard againft my ftick, the ball of my hand fuffered very much. It is more centrical than Skiddow, and the fpring is a treafure; perhaps the diffi-culty we furmounted tended to make us think it the monarch of Britifh moun-tains, for we certainly call it fo. I be-lieve mankind in general is inclined to feel the recollection of paft labour more fatisfactory than paft eafe; and, as I am feated quietly in my own chamber fome time after having finifhed my ramble, Helvellyn increafes in favour every day.

Q 2   Although

Although we afcended many hills higher than Helm Crag, as it has never been vifited by ftrangers, and the afcent is fo very difficult, I think it deferves being mentioned in fpeaking of mountains.

Many of the mountains we journeyed over before we reached Helvellyn, and in the road to Buttermere and Patterdale, were noble ones; but, for want of a guide, I cannot diftinguifh their names.

CHAP.

CHAP. XXXIII.

Caſtle Hill—Aſhneſs Rock—Hutton the Guide—His Reſearches—His Gratitude—Keſwick Bellman.

CASTLE Hill commands both lakes, and is ſo near Keſwick, we would recommend thoſe who have not time to mount Skiddow not to fail viſiting it. We afterwards walked through a ſhady lane to Barrow caſcade, which in this dry ſeaſon has much the advantage of its neighbour, the boaſted Lowdore. We went round the pleaſure-ground, and ſaw ſome valuable oaks, ſuch as ought to cover our waſte land ; many hundred thouſand acres of which ſtill bear the name of foreſts, without producing one tree. I think there is much ſatisfaction in looking at

Q 3   young

young plantations, as to future navies; and every lover of his country ought to regret when he fees a woodlefs foreft. We came out near a bridge, which put us with little trouble in the way to Afh-nefs rock. Planting ourfelves under a fhade, we overlook Lowdore into the gorge of Barrowdale; a turn of the head gives the ferpentine river to Grange bridge, terminating with a well-cloathed clump, and rugged mountains * over-hanging it, and which we had paffed over in our excurfion to Buttermere.

We have the fame fight of Baffen-thwaite as we had from Caftle Hill, with the advantage of taking in the extenfive range from Walloh Crag.

As we called it rather an idle morn-ing, we went to Hutton's Mufeum. He has all the minerals, fpars, and rocks of

* Over one of which a young mountaineer miftook his way two months ago, and was dafhed to pieces.

the

the mountains, and a very well-chofen botanical collection. My friend added a new fhilling and fix-pence to his coins, which look very bright amongft the rufty Romans; and, as he faid, " would be a " fine fight for the country people." The poor fellow did not know how to make amends for the little we did for him; and he told us, with tears in his eyes, " Gentlemen, I don't really know how to thank you, but I'll tell you what I'll do —I'll fend you frefh char, whenever you want it, as cheap as I get it myfelf."

His merit and modefty (as far as we could judge) keep pace with each other, and he feems to deferve encouragement. He toils day and night, during the fea-fon, at the defire of ftrangers, and is ju-dicioufly acquainted with Mr. Weft's ftations, having often been with him when he fixed upon them. In winter he is either fcrutinizing the hills for fof-

Q 4   fils,

fils, or in bad weather following the humble occupation of a weaver; and, what adds greatly to his merit, he never received but one quarter's fchooling.

Some people have expreffed themfelves diffatisfied with his fmall houfe and his little Mufeum. Poor fellow ! he has not money enough to make them larger. It is a very improper mode of judging; they fhould recollect, if he has a little Mufeum, he has but a little fortune ; and if he has a fmall houfe, he has a large family. Think thus, ye travellers, who are journeying to pleafe yourfelves; and furely a fhilling will not be thrown away on Hutton's Mufeum. This is the man-ner my friend thought, and for every thing this civil man did for us his fhil-lings became larger pieces.

Whilft we were at his houfe, Crofs-thwaite, the bellman, went by ; we were

taking

taking notice how diftinctly he fpoke; and were told, he had been married fixty-five years to his prefent wife, has had many children, apprentices *, and fervants, yet never had one death in his family.

* He was once a reputable fhoe-maker.

CHAP.

CHAP. XXXIV.

The Effect of Echo on the Lake—An Irishman's Account of the Lake of Killarney.

IT was a calm evening, and Hutton took a large wall-piece in his boat. We tried three difcharges. The echoes anfwered by rufhing from feveral hills, and then died away amidft the rocks of Barrowdale. I do not pretend to defcribe the vibration, nor how long it continued: if I was to fay near a minute, fome people might think I exaggerated; but thofe who have heard it on an equally fine evening would fay I do not fpeak with juftice if I did not allow it upwards of thirty feconds.

When

When we were oppofite Walloh Crag, Hutton, with a fhrill call, produced five diftinct echoes, and they died away with the tremble of an Æolian harp. Let the Lake-fanciers make the experiment, and they will be amply gratified, perhaps more on this lake than on any other; the fituation of the mountains, with the rough tops of fome of them, are well calculated for effect, the diftances being neither too great, nor too confined.

I was lounging about the head of the lake, waiting for my party, and faw two fifhermen turning it; one was better dreffed than the other, and, by the motion of his right hand, feemed to be abufing him; he ftopped frequently, and then darted forward. Curiofity induced me to go nearer, and I obferved the *Antonio* of the other evening; and, by the extended mouth of the countryman, he was taking in one of the fineft fpeeches

ever

ever rehearſed ; but, what muſt be of
more conſequence to the theatrical hero,
they had caught many fiſh, and I ſuppoſe the idea of a good ſupper filled him
with imaginary greatneſs,

A boat full of ſervants ſoon afterwards
went jovially off : a man came running
to the beach, and hollowed after them to
take him in : they either would not hear
him, or did not chuſe to mind him. He
expreſſed his diſappointment with ſome
oaths : but, as I thought it was hard he
ſhould loſe his opportunity, I deſired him
to ſtep forward into our boat.

" Bleſſings thank you now ; I'll give
" you a hand at a pull of an oar if you
" want one." I told him we were going
to hear the effect of an echo. " Echoes !
" —why there is not ſuch an echo in
" all the world as Killarney's ; it will
" anſwer you fairly nine times."

We

We rowed towards Hubert's Ifland, and made the firft difcharge about Silver Hill. I afked the Irifhman if he did not think it was equal to Killarney's, for it anfwered more than nine times :—" No, " no, Sir, no! for, befides the nine times, " there is *nine anfwers* to it :" but he al-lowed, when he had heard Cormorant Rocks againft Walloh Crag, " By Jafus I " never heard any thing like *that* in all my " life :" and I dare venture to fay, as he is going over the water, Kefwick's fair lake will rebound nine times nine, allow-ing for reverberating diftance.

CHAP.

CHAP. XXXV.

OBSERVATIONS.

Remarks and Observations, previous to lea-
ving the Lakes, which, I hope, may not
be deemed intruding.

IN anſwer to ſome queſtions made to a
gentleman reſiding in the North, I have
the pleaſure of tranſcribing part of a letter, which will introduce ſome honeſt
cuſtoms, that cannot fail proving ac-
ceptable to ſtrangers.

" The queſtion you aſk, reſpecting the
" blackſmiths, was almoſt univerſal with-
" in my memory. The neighbours, on
" an appointed day, went with their
" horſes and carts, and conveyed as
" many coals, *gratis*, as were ſufficient
" for

" for one year's confumption; this was
" generally done in the Spring, previous
" to the commencement of their tillage,
" that poor Vulcan might have no
" excufe for idlenefs, or neglect, from
" want of fuel, and that every inhabitant
" might have his plough-fhare and coul-
" ter properly fharpened againft the ex-
" igent time; thus you will obferve, that
" accommodation was mixed with cha-
" rity. It gives me pain to remark,
" that this laudable cuftom is banifhed
" from what WE efteem our more *po-*
" *lifhed places.* At the fame time I am
" happy to obferve, the cuftom is ftill
" preferved in the more fequeftered parts,
" where primitive poverty, and unaf-
" fected manners, prevail over modern
" refinement.

" The cuftom of prefenting donations
" at the marriages of all ranks and de-
" grees in the North is ftill in ufe, but
" more fo among the lower order.
" Every

" Every neighbour, and all the kinsfolk,
" prefent fomething, according to their
" ability—half a dozen pewter plates,
" half a dozen knives and forks, candle-
" fticks, tea-kettle, bedding, and vari-,
" ous other articles of furniture ; fo that
" a poor bride, upon the day of her
" nuptials, has a houfe comfortably fur-
" nifhed. Pity but fuch a cuftom fhould
" become univerfal.

" A fervant girl, who has continued in
" the fame fervitude feven years, is en-
" titled upon her marriage to a copper
" kettle, generally containing from four
" to fix gallons ; this is always prefented,
" except the bride chufes fome other
" equivalent in lieu of it.

" Another remarkable cuftom at chrif-
" tenings ftill prevails in the dales of
" the North. Upon the day of celebra-
" ting the ceremony, all the matrons in
" the neighbourhood affemble at the joy-
" ful

" ful houfe, and each brings as a pre-
" fent, to the good woman in the ftraw,
" either a pound of fugar, a pound of
" butter, or fix-penny-worth of wheaten
" bread. The bread is cut in thin flices,
" and placed in rows one above another,
" in a large kettle of twenty or thirty
" gallons. The butter and fugar are
" diffolved in a feparate one, and then
" poured upon the bread, where it con-
" tinues until it has boiled for fome
" fpace, and the bread is perfectly fa-
" turated with the mixture; it is then
" taken out, and ferved up by way of de-
" fert. This curious difh is called *But-*
" *tered Sops.*

" You make mention in your Ramble
" of the young farmers acting plays du-
" ring the Winter; thefe, by way of
" diftinction, were called *Speech-plays.*
" I remember a country lad, of the name
" of Crighton, was performing in a co-
" medy; the name does not at this in-
" ftant occur. However, he was on the

R   " point

" point of detecting his wife with her
" gallant. He should have made his en-
" try with caution, and with the follow-
" ing sentence aside :—' *I'll spoil your*
" *intrigues* ;'—but, instead of whispering
" it, he bounced upon the stage with
" the violence of a madman, and, with
" vociferation equal to Richard offering
" his Kingdom for his Horse, exclaimed
" with stentorian lungs—' *I'll spoil your*
" IN-TRI-GUES,'—articulating every syl-
" lable, to the no small diversion of the
" audience. Another time performing
" in a farce, and ranting as usual, the
" following words occurred as in italics
" *(and then he gave a start)*. Not content
" with exerting his usual force of lungs,
" he bounced across the stage with
" the agility Harlequin darts through a
" trap-door to avoid his pursuers ; and
" the laughter occasioned was felt as ap-
" plause.

" A celebrated and very ingenious pro-
" filist, residing in London, early in life
                                    " com-

" commenced actor, manager, and au-
" thor. I recollect the two firft lines of
" a prologue, written and fpoken by
" himfelf, which, for their novelty, de-
" ferve to be remembered, not as a *norma*
" *fcribendi,* but as a literary curiofity :

> " From little *Strickland* I do came,
> " And am a moft delightful fwain.

" Anecdotes of thefe kinds are in
" abundance, but, when they cannot be
" appropriated, lofe much of their effect;
" yet they are often fpoken of in our re-
" tired fituations, with good-humoured
" remembrance, long after the authors
" have ceafed to be inhabitants of this
" world."

With the gentleman who favoured me
with the above, we muft regret, when
refinement, or what may not be impro-
perly called *the tinfel of it*—fhould wear
away cuftoms that confolidated fuch ufeful links in fmall fociety—and we muft

R 2 look

look with veneration upon thofe primitive retreats that ftill preferve them.

After fuch addition to the OBSERVATIONS, I chearfully and without apology return to the remarks given in the firft edition—and truft I may not be thought prefuming, by offering fome general obfervations on leaving Kefwick for a larger town; which have been thus long deferred that I might fpeak with authenticity. Follow me, Reader, and hear what I have to fay. I am amongft a people who are too much my fuperiors to have juftice done them. I declare, although I have been a tolerably great traveller, I never met fo unaffuming or obliging fet of human beings before; and I congratulate my country on their belonging to it. I will fay thus far of ourfelves; had we chofen, we might have got introductions to the firft gentlemen in the counties; but we preferred a more humble walk, and were amply repaid for it.

The

The inhabitants in general about thefe mountainous countries are not fo tall or lufty as in many others; perhaps, as it requires great induftry to get a livelihood, the growth of their children is checked by early labour. They live to a very advanced age; the faces of the very old are ftrong and healthfully marked with deep fhort wrinkles. The middle-aged are commonly handfome; their youth are ruddy and fun-burnt; their children have the faces of cherubs, and feemed to have " the milk of Dorothy" flowing purely in their veins.

They are not only affectionate to their parents, but friendly amongft each other; and a man would run a rifk of his life in deep fnow *, in venturing over the fteepeft mountains to attend the funeral of a friend. They have the higheft re-

* As Robert Newton did, over a mountain he had never paffed before.

R 3

fpect

fpect for the dead, perhaps to a degree bordering upon fuperftition; and they rather rob the living by the expence they put themfelves to at a funeral: but, as a livelihood, not a love of gain, is their grand confideration, they are too friendly and induftrious to want; and I did not fee (except the little vagrants at Kef-wick) one perfon that afked for charity.

Their food is homely. They prefer a thin oat-cake to wheat-bread; and they are fond of the natural products of the earth, which may be the reafon of feeing a large family in every houfe, for we did not call at a cottage that had lefs than three children. Their drink confifts of butter-milk and whey, and occafionally a draught of ftout ale. Spirits are feldom ufed to excefs; their baneful influence is almoft unknown; they are taken as cordials, and I hope they will never make farther encroachment; but it is dangerous to truft them. The Queen of Patterdale fets her fubjects a bad example, and will

pro-

probably foon fall a victim to an unfortunate ufe of them.

They are as good fcholars as the Scottifh peafantry; and though the lower order of the people in the South might think them their inferiors, I will be bound, they would puzzle them at *hic*, *hæc*, *hoc*, and in juftnefs of obfervation. They are always ready to do a good turn to a ftranger, and, inftead of expecting money for any trifling affiftance, will take off their hats, throw their heads at you, and wifh you a good day. If this example was to make its way fouthward, it would be of fervice; for their rapacioufnefs to ftrangers is a difgrace to the country. I was lately in a gentleman's phaëton, in Kent, when a piece of the harnefs gave way. A man, with feeming civility and good-nature, lent us affiftance, though it was not wanted; and, when he had done, the gentleman thanked him. He threw his hat on his head, changed his civility of counte-

R 4

nance

nance into a frown, and faid, " D——
" your thanks, if that's all."—I will tell
you what a man in the North would
have faid, "Sur, con I affift ho?—there's
" no deanger—gud day to hoa."

In Kendal there are many Quakers,
and about Penrith fome Roman Catho-
licks; but, immediately in the villages
near the Lakes, they are all of the Eftablifhed Church. The have no Metho-
difts, or new-fangled doctrines, to dif-
turb them. I afked a man what they
would do with a Methodift if he was to
preach amongft them? " Turn him out;
" we're content with our own parfon,
" and th' church is large enough to
" houd us aw." This was at Grafsmere,
and I felt much pleafure at his remark,
for I dare fay there is not a town in England that has not been rendered more
uncomfortable in proportion as they give
way to field enthufiafm.

I had

I had the curiofity, in paffing through Nottingham, to hear a young brawny zealot, who was brawling away a heap of nonfenfe to a gaping crowd under the New Change in the market-place. I never heard the Scriptures fo diftorted, and, I dare fay, there were more hearers than would attend afternoon's fervice at church.

Is it not difgraceful, that it fhould be allowed in a part of the town that is under the immediate protection of the magiftrates?

The clerk was a thin-gutted contraft— the very look Wefton ufed to put on in Doctor Laft, when he returns for his fhoes, with the addition of the face being more lengthened either by religion or hypocrify. The brawler had fometimes his hand on this *curious head*; and fometimes feemed to point to him as a fanctimonious example.

There

There cannot be a fairer proof of the foundnefs of our Religion than the harmlefs lives the inhabitants of the Lakes live. The mountains around them not only preferve it undifturbed, but ferve as barriers to keep out many follies and vices, which are afloat amongft people that unjuftly think themfelves more enlightened.

The country gentlemen give the poor leave to angle in the lakes and rivers, and they often take more than fupplies their families. Net-fifhing is farmed, and char is never caught by the hook. This fifh frequents the deepeft part of the Lakes, and is only found in fome of them; Windermere, Coniftone, and Buttermere, are the beft fupplied; many are totally without, although they have communication with lakes that abound with them; and, notwithftanding Ullfwater is as deep as Windermere, they do not thrive fo well in it, but are of equal flavour.

Small.

Small quantities are taken in Haws-wa-ter. Pike are not found in Ullfwater; but a particular fpecies of trout, called the grey trout, is almoft peculiar to it-felf: it is beaked like a falmon, and of vaft bulk; fome have been taken from thirty to forty pounds, of a very delicate tafte. Perch and trout are abundant every where; and pike are in general common; but, what is a circumftance too remarkable to omit, when char quit Windermere to fpawn, they go up the fame neck of water with the trout, and then take to the Brathay, the trout to the Rathay.

In mowing they juft cut fufficient for a family to work, as they have few hands, and the weather is not to be depended upon. The mower does not bend low to his fcythe, but takes a long fweep, then raifes himfelf very erect, until the back of the fcythe touches his hams. I think the motion full as graceful as that made ufe of by the failors in the Mediterranean when

when rowing ; and it would be as much admired, if it was a foreign cuftom inftead of a North-of-England one. After it is mown, they fhake it with their hands ; and, as it is moftly fine grafs, if the weather proves favourable it is houfed the next day ; fometimes carrying it home in fmall carts, fometimes on horfeback or wheelbarrows, or, when they have more children than money, by haycocks faftened on a man's fhoulders like a knapfack. They then proceed upon another plot, and are indefatigable until it is dark, which does not always put a period to their labour.

The woods, which add greatly to the witchcraft of the country, and to the wealth of their owners, are cut down in about fourteen years ; fo you may obferve the progreffive growth, beginning on the fecond year with a head as curly as the Africans. Thefe copfes are beautified with various trees, and with one I never faw in the South, the round-leafed alder,

alder, which ferves to make wooden-
fhoes, not fuch as were worn in France,
that pinched fo feverely in the days of
defpotifm; nor yet fuch as are fo extended at this period of their unbridled
licentioufnefs, but fuch as are well calculated for an induftrious people to trudge
dry-fhod through marfhy grounds; and,
by way of making them laft longer, they
bind them with plates of iron.

Nuts and apples are this year fcarce,
and the fruit in general fmall and ill-
tafted; but, even if they were as good as
they could be, you would be made welcome, for they never put themfelves to the
expence of having a garden-lock. Their
fuel confifts of peat and turf; the fmell
of which is uncomfortable to thofe un-
accuftomed to it. This fuel occafions
fuch a cloud of fmoke, it looks picturefque iffuing from a neat-cottage, with
a contraft of wood and water near it.

Groufe

254 A Fortnight's Ramble

Grouse is not so plentiful as it used to be. The countrymen say, it is owing to the strictness of the land-owners, as there are more birds of prey than formerly, which are greater poachers and lamb-destroyers than man. A certain sum is given for every eagle or raven that is killed. This is a dangerous undertaking; for they are obliged to be let over the mountains by ropes, and the eagle fights hard in defence of its nest *, nor could it be taken if the man was not to cover himself with wool to entangle the claws.

There are very few small birds. These tit-bits are soon destroyed by the number of becks and claws which are after them. Those we did see seemed afraid to shew themselves, and burrowed in the thick foliage, as if they had been

* There are never more than two eggs in an eagle's nest, and one is generally addled.

5   ac-

accuftomed to keep a good look-out; but I did not hear one fongfter during the tour, except a lonefome lark in Buttermere, and that fcarcely for a minute. Crifpin, the guide, faid they had many of them in the fpring, and fpoke as if he thought there had not been any of them in the fouthern parts of England; in fhort, out of his own valley, where all his ideas feemed to be concentered.

The high roads are in general in excellent repair, and the commons well fupplied with finger-pofts. A road once made will laft a long while; the firft expence is heavy, but they are not burthened by after-repairs, or the traveller by turnpikes.

I do not think his Majefty has more loyal fubjects in his dominions; and, if Mr. PITT fhould caft a look upon this humble production, I have the fatisfaction

tion of telling him, the *Proclamation* was upon all the church-doors, and they looked as clean as the day they were put up, except that we could fometimes trace the mark of a finger that had con-ned it over. But why need I mention this? I make no doubt he already knows it; for I faw Mr. Bellingham, who was once one of his private fecretaries, in a fmall town, making remarks upon a droll fporting fign; and of courfe every thing he faw, which was of national con-fequence, would get to *head quarters* at laft.

The air upon the mountains is fo clear, I fancied myfelf as brifk as the fheep around me; and the hilarity I en-joyed was fuch as I have felt after drink-ing champaigne, with the difference of a longer continuance without the relax-ation it occafions. A certain gaiety per-vades me at the recollection, and I truft it will pleafure my fancy when-

ever

ever it burfts upon my memory. I am affured, whatever I wrote upon thofe noble elevations are as faithfully delineated as my time would allow; my eye ran over them with a dafh of perfpicuity, and indelibly fixed their beauties in the mind.

S   CHAR,

CHAP. XXXVI.

The Road to Penrith—The Beacon—Rich Country—The Borderers—The Caftle.

As we afcended the hill towards Penrith, idly feated in a chaife, we took a parting fight of the Lake, and I even thought the houfe on the ifland looked well. We then paffed along the vale of *Threlkeld*, with feveral miles of delightful profpects and good road, until we came upon an extenfive common, famous for drearinefs and large flocks of geefe. As we had been regaled for fome time with variety, I thought it a good opportunity to enjoy the pleafures of retrofpection, and was again amidft the fcenes we had left. I was brufhing the morning dew, and returning at evening with

with my mind full of the day—I was attending Echo with its beſt effects—I was laughing at the Iriſhman—and enjoying a bowl of whey in a cottage—a confounded jolt awoke me from my reverie.

By degrees, a fine country opened, and at the twelfth mile-ſtone we ſaw the hoſpitable roof of Greyſtock Caſtle. The land kept improving, and corn-fields began to ſhew their yellow heads; tall aſh-trees kept the ſun from us; and at twelve we entered Penrith, on a market-day, rendered more buſy, from the biſhop of Carliſle holding his viſitation and confirmation.

Penrith * is a handſome town; many of the houſes are built of a reddiſh ſtone; it would be a great improvement if they would pull down their ſhambles, and ſome old houſes, which diſgrace an otherwiſe-good market-place.

* Penrith ſignifies, in the Britiſh, *Red Hill*, and hath its name from the hill of red ſtone adjoining.

S 2   I went

I went in the afternoon upon the Beacon, and had a fine champaign country all around, with waving corn upon it, as thick as in any part of England. I had no perfon with me to defcribe the different views; but I could obferve this hill was well fituated to overlook the incurfions made by the borderers in days of difcord, and to give fignals to the many caftles fcattered about in order to make a *fortie* upon them, or for the people to retire to when the enemy was too powerful.

I felt with fatisfaction, that the rich fields, far as the eye could reach, would not only fupply the inhabitants with bread, but produce a granary that could furnifh an extent of country with that divine gift.

I faw part of Ullfwater, and many of the mountains we had left. As it is a very eafy afcent, do not fail going upon it; the fides are beautifully purpled, and there

there are feveral quarries of red ftone, from which they have built the church.

I then croffed the Eamont, and walked to the caftle, a ruin in its laft ftage; it has been encircled by a ditch, with two draw-bridges, and is faid to have been built by Henry the Sixth, and was the refidence, for a fhort time, of Richard the Third. It is dilapidating very faft. The rude hands of Ignorance and Rapacioufnefs have been more deftructive to it than time, and, ere long, the fite only will remain. The mind has a certain feel of forrow in feeing the poor foundation of a once-noble caftle that has been torn afunder; and the owner of fuch property degrades himfelf, who permits it to be ufed for park-walls, barns, or modern houfes. It is from fuch falfe tafte that our grandeft ruins have been hurried to decay, and the reverence we owe to our anceftors has been leffened.

S 3　　　　CHAP.

CHAP. XXXVII.

The Church—Ravages of the Plague—Antient Stones in the Church-Yard—Vulgar Opinion about them—Respect for the Grave of an old Woman.

ON the morrow, an old gentleman, near eighty, who was churchwarden when the Scotch went through in 1745, amused us with many stories of that day; they had made a deep impression, and are of course often repeated. He civilly went with me into the church *, which

was

---

* This church was built in the years 1720, 1721, 1722. At this time, Dr. Hugh Todd was vicar, who, although a man of exemplary piety and great erudition, yet his deportment amongst his parishioners was haughty and supercilious in the extreme, which consequently

gave

was rebuilt early in this century, except
the fteeple, which is the antient one.

I wrote down the following account,
from a ftone near the communion-table,
of the numbers that perifhed by the
plague in 1598.

In Penrith   2260.
Kendal   2500.
Richmond   2200.
Carlifle   1196.

gave offence; injured the caufe of morality, and rendered
his literary acquifitions of fmall reputation among his
flock. A wag, who probably thought himfelf the Martial of his day, wrote the following epigram, more re-
markabie, probably, for its truth and farcaftic turn,
than for its wit or refinement, which he affixed to the
church-door.

" A new church,
And an old fteeple;
A proud prieft,
And a perverfe people."

S 4   There

There is a bounding-ftone in the country, where provifions were daily left for
the fufferers.

Penrith muft have been confiderably
more populous than it is at prefent; for,
it does not contain more inhabitants
than perifhed by that dreadful fcourge.
The church is handfome, and the lower
pillars are compofed of fingle ftones,
three yards and a half in height. Some
of the windows have remnants of paintings, that were taken from the old ones ;
and there are two plain brafs chande-
liers, with infcriptions round them, mentioning they are the gift of the Duke of
Cumberland, in remembrance of the
loyalty of the town, in 1745.

In the church-yard there are two pyra-
midical ftones, about four yards afunder,
with four odd-fhaped ones in the feparation, all of them of hard ftone, except
one, which is the red ftone, and, from

6   being

being fofter, is reduced to half the fize of the others. You may juft diftinguifh remnants of hieroglyphics on one of them; and as one ftone is fhaped fomething like the back of a boar, and as this country was in the midft of a foreft, it may be the monument of a man famous for deftroying them *.

I could get no intelligence of its antiquity; vulgar opinion fpeaks of it as the burial-place of an extraordinary-fized

* The people have a tradition, that a famous knighterrant, one Sir Ewan Cæfarius, was buried here, who, in his time, made a mighty havock amongſt thofe beaſts in Inglewood foreſt. Mr. Page, who was fchoolmaſter at Penrith from 1581 to 1591, has in his writings left this memorandum: that a ſtranger-gentleman coming to an inn there defired to have fome of the principal inhabitants to fup with him, whereupon Mr. Page and fome others attended him. The ſtranger told them, he came to fee the antiquities of the place; and, drawing out a paper, faid, that Sir Hugh Cæfarius had an hermitage fomewhere thereabouts, called Sir Hugh's Parlour; and this place was fome time afterwards opened by one William Turner, who there found the great long fhank-bones of a man, and a broad fword.

man,

man, and the feparation is meant for his height. I afked feveral people about it, and found that every one had a myfterious opinion of his own ; but, as the *wonderful* makes the eafieft impreffions on vacant minds, his antediluvian fize has many favourers. However, induced by curiofity, they have lately dug to the depth of fix yards, without meeting any trace to reward the refearch. The above remark was made in confequence of enquiries on the fpot. The interefting note on the other fide was fent me by the Reverend Mr. Holme.

There is likewife a fingle ftone as antient as the others. I left thefe obfcure antiques, and found, not far from them, a brafs plate againft the church, near the grave of Alice Atkinfon, aged 112 ; and felt more refpect in treading over her remains than upon the others, which probably contain no other proof of antiquity than what is above ground.

I

CHAP.

CHAP. XXXVIII.

ULLSWATER.

Ullfwatei Lake—Firft Arm of it—Singular Prefervation of a Man and his Horfe— Martindale Valley and Fells—Famous for the Wild Stag—Grand Appearance of Helvellyn—Gowborough Park—Deer, Cattle, &c.

WE took a chaife to Ullfwater, to accommodate our obliging old gentleman, and had a charming ride by the banks of the Eamont. We paffed through Mr. Haffel's park, in front of a handfome ftone houfe. On opening the right wing, the garden has a ftriking effect. The grounds are irregular, and have an excellent object in Dunmallart Head. We

rounded

rounded the bottom of this hill, still
beautiful, though despoiled of many trees;
it is so regularly cut down, it reminded
me of the shaved heads of the Hindoos.
It was once a Roman station, as I make
no doubt every hill was in this part of
the country that is at the entrance of a
valley; but the numbers of works carried on upon them centuries ago have
obliterated every trace of them.

We procured a boat; and I will begin
by our setting off. The low hills to the
right were covered with sheep and cattle, that were lashing their sides on the
summit, and the sky seen under their
bellies gives a beautiful and delineating
shape of them: neat houses were scat-
tered along the banks. The left looks
naked, but variegated with some cottages, and the green reward of their labour around them: these are overtopped
by steep fells. When you reach the first
arm, Swarth Fell appears rugged and
steep.

This

This mountain will always be remembered by the providential efcape of the father of the prefent Mr. Haffel. Being in a fox-chace on its fummit, his eagernefs threw him into a fituation that rendered it impoffible for him to return. He therefore difmounted, and preffed as clofe as poffible to his horfe; thus fupporting each other through this perilous ftage, they arrived fafe at the bottom, in prefence of many fpectators, and where no perfon was ever known before or fince to have defcended.

The horfe is remembered as well as the man; and WHITE STOCKINGS was permitted to range the reft of her life, with the beft fodder and attention a grateful mafter could beftow upon her.

Oppofite to Swarth Fell there is a farm-houfe upon the fite of an old church, the ground about it being the rich elbow we admired when upon Helvellyn. From the

the line of wildnefs on the left you open
the lively vale of Martindale, whofe fells
are famous for the wild ftag.   In Water
Nook we fired a fmall canon, and heard
an echo which might have been to-
lerable if we had not been upon Kefwick Lake. We then made Gowborough
Park * an objeét, whofe plain and fides
were full of deer; innumerable cattle
being on the borders of the lake, and
cooling themfelves in it.

We had a fuperb view of Helvellyn,
rearing his broad fhoulders over many
hills. The mind cannot conceive a more
folemn fight; and the imagination would
be too much ftretched, if you were not to
turn your head to the vale of Martindale,
which is as fmiling as verdure can make
it.

* Gowborough Park, confifting of eighteen hundred
acres, and ftocked with upwards of fix hundred head
of deer.

CHAP.

CHAP. XXXIX.

ULLSWATER.

Lyulph's Tower—Duke of Norfolk—Style of Living there—The Cafcade—Shape of the Lake—King Arthur's round Table— A modern Shrubbery—Why Ullfwater Lake exceeds the others.

WE landed near Lyulph's Tower, whofe rugged walls fo fuitably anfwer the fcenes around it. I muft again mention the Duke of Norfolk; for, when here, he never ufes chairs, but wooden forms, and has a long hofpitable board for a table.

The four towers have fine profpects from them; but, I was forry to fee the

rain

rain had committed great depredation, owing to the rugged building of the walls, or perhaps becaufe it was done by contract.

We afcended to the waterfall, through a thick wood that hangs along the path, until you come to a bridge that might have *grown* in its fituation. After fpeaking of the incomparable Scale Force, I did not intend faying more of cafcades ; but this, though fparing of water, is only exceeded by *one* of the prides of Buttermere ; for we muft not forget the fair Sally as the firft. The bridge*, the road, the feat, every thing that art has added, appear as if they were formed by Nature.

I croffed the oppofite brow, and looked into the bafin that receives the water from a diminutive fall. I then

* The bridge, a friend tells me, was foon afterwards wafhed away.

bent

bent my way to within a mile of the fpot where I had made remarks from the Amblefide journey. I could here fee the formation of the lake, with the three iflands; and had a good peep into Pat-terdale.

Ullfwater is fhaped like the letter Z made by a bad penman: when we faw it from Helvellyn, the top arm was not vifible, which occafioned its looking like a pair of breeches.

We reimbarked at four, after trying another difcharge. I dare fay it would have had a fine effect, had the day been fufficiently calm. The rufhes from Place Fell were loud, but the wind took away the departing found. Clouds were gathering on the head mountains, and, as we left them under a frefh fail, they were foftened by the diftance. After we came to the old church, the farm was a neat object, and we had a chearful fight of Dunmallart Head.

T We

We returned to Penrith on the village fide of the Eamont, along narrow fhaded lanes, until we came to Eamont Bridge, near which is a plot of ground called King Arthur's Round Table *, a place where tournaments, in days of chivalry, are traditioned by the country people to have been held; the two approaches whence we will fuppofe the champions entered the lift are ftill vifible, and you may mark out accommodations for the fpectators. According to my ideas of thofe extravagancies, they could not poffibly exceed the reprefentation of them at the Hay-market; at leaft fo I thought; and I care not if I infringe upon the laws of chivalry by the comparifon.

* Rapin, in his encomium upon Arthur, page 39, fays, " He is faid to have inftituted the ORDER OF THE " KNIGHTS OF THE ROUND TABLE, fo famous in ro- " mances. Though this inftitution has given occafion " for many fabulous relations, it is not therefore to be " deemed altogether chimerical."

In

In the evening we went with the good old gentleman into a fhrubbery * ; and, though fo old, he walked ftoutly to the laft.—I forget the name of the place. Afh feems to thrive particularly well; one tree is the ftraighteft I ever faw. You have good commanding views— you fee a caftle † built by the countefs of Pembroke—Penrith caftle, and Helvellyn heights. The river winds through the grounds broad and clear, with a mill beautified into an object.

I was glad to get out of the fhrubbery; for fhrubberies are plentiful in the South of England, and my head was too full of mountains, lakes, and valleys, to wifh to be interrupted by the moft perfect pleafure-ground in the world. I am not yet far enough from the wild fcenes of

* Suppofed to be Bird Neft, from the profpect it afforded.

† Brougham Caftle.

T 2

Na-

Nature, to be pleafed with any thing that is ftudied.

Much as I admired the other lakes, I cannot help giving preference to Ullf-water : every arm prefents new beauties —Helvellyn—the interior mountains—the village and plain of Patterdale—Place Fell—the iflands—the tower—Gowbo-rough Park—the vale of Martindale—the rough mountains, and the fertile ones —Dunmallart Head—Yes! every houfe, from Water Milloch to the pooreft cottage, appears in its proper place, without difpleafing the eye by attempts at finery ; and there is a chaftenefs about the whole, that makes it the choiceft gift of Nature I ever faw.

CHAP.

CHAP. XL.

*Leave Penrith—Carpet Manufactory—A
Collection of Timber—Of Hayſtacks—
Knipe Scarr—Vale and Village of Bamp-
ton—Hawſwater Lake—Bampton Free-
School—A Village-School a good Nurſery
for Morals—Druidical Stones at Shap—
The Abbey—The Concluſion—A Copy of
Verſes.*

LEFT Penrith, to go to Shap ; ſent forward the carriage, whilſt we went to look
at a regular-built village, which is but
thinly inhabited ; many of the houſes are
unfiniſhed, and there were cattle in ſome
of them. We afterwards walked to a
carpet manufactory under the inſpection
of Mr. Bloom. It is beautiful in the extreme, in point of colouring, and the

T 3 thick-

thicknefs of the work ; and is a credit to the patronizer, not only for the workman-fhip, but for the employment given to many orphans taken from the Foundling Hofpital ; however, he has a large ftock on hand.

We proceeded through Lowther Park. The houfe was burnt down in the late Lord's time. There is a confiderable depofit of timber intended to be ufed in the rebuilding of it, which was buried many years under ground, but is now thatched over. Oppofite there are the greateft quantity and the largeft hay-ftacks I ever faw.

On Knipe Scarr there are plantations of thick pines confpicuous throughout the country ; this command overlooks the vale and village of Bampton, a val-ley beautifully fcattered with farm-houfes. We then followed the road to Rofe-Gill Head, where we have a foftened view of the vale, and a pleafant fight of Hawf-water.

water. As well as I can judge (for we had only a fifh-pond fight of it), it is fur-rounded by woody hills, and rich mea-dows overtopped by fells. After the water has left the lake, it forms a bold cafcade at Thornthwaite Mill, and then runs by the town.

The Free-fchool of Bampton not only gives education to the neighbours, but has produced men who have been con-fpicuous in the world. Bifhop Gibfon and Judge Wilfon received the rudi-ments of their education here; and fe-veral whom we may rank amongft our London merchants, and, if not in as ex-alted, in as ufeful and honourable a line of life as any our country can boaft of.

A good fchool in a quiet valley is well calculated to engraft the moft falutary impreffions on a young mind. Uncon-taminated by bad example, he has only to attend to good; for, every one around him is almoft as innocent as himfelf, or,

T 4 what

what approaches near to it, whatever is bad is difcountenanced.

When he has laid in his little ftock, which generally confifts of juft enough of Latin to make him underftand Englifh grammatically, a thorough knowledge of accompts, and writing a good hand, he is qualified to be of fervice to the merchant and to himfelf. He learns that induftry is a perpetual recommendation; and, from not having a fufficiency of fortune to be idle (even were he inclined to it), his perfeverance paves the way to future fuccefs.

When he arrives in London, he has a *rough polifh*—if I may be allowed the expreffion. The *roughnefs* is the dialect, which gradually lofes its harfhnefs, and, in proportion as you value the man, wears quite away. The *polifh* is a found-principled education, which can never be obliterated : it not only ferves as a check to youthful faults, but is the Mentor which

which hinders them from growing into habits, and the pilot that reftores the erring mind to its village rectitude.

Numbers of Druidical-ftones * (or, as fome people fay, in honour of Danifh heroes)

* " Thefe ftones are certainly Druidical; they occupy an area upwards of half a mile in length, and between twenty and thirty yards in breadth; they ftand nearly parallel to each other, rather rounding at the top. Many of them are three or four yards in diameter, at eight, ten, or twelve yards diftance, which are of fuch immenfe weight that no carriage now in ufe could fupport them. Undoubtedly this has been a place of Druid worfhip, as it is known they always performed in the open air, within this kind of inclofure, fhaded with wood, as this place in antient times appears to have been, although there is fcarce a tree to be feen (Shap Thorn only excepted, planted on the top of the hill for the direction of travellers). At the high end of this place of worfhip, there is a circle of the like ftones, about eighteen feet in diameter, which was their *Sanctum Sanctorum*, and place of worfhip. The ftone is a kind of granite, and when broken appears beautifully variegated with bright fhining fpots like fpar. The country people have blafted and carried away fome of thefe ftones for the foundation-ftones of buildings. The building of
Shap

heroes) are fcattered about Shap. They
are different from the mother-ftone of
the neighbourhood; yet they feem too
large to have been brought by art, and
too carelefs on the furface to have been
formed there.

Shap Abbey was built in 1158, and has
been difmantled to build paltry houfes.
Part of the fteeple, with trees upon it
that have withered with age, and cells
under the once body of the abbey, are
the only remains of this ruin; it has been
fhamefully deftroyed. A fine ftream runs
near it, and the ground produces fweet
grafs, and hay that is all fragrance!

There has been a bridge near the abbey, but it has been forced away by torrents, and you are obliged to ftep over
the remains in vifiting thefe ruins from
Shap village. The monaftic fathers ge-

Shap abbey was no injury to this fine piece of antiquity,
being entirely built of free-ftone from a neighbouring
quarry.

7   nerally

nerally chofe fertile fituations, which
gives us the liberty of thinking they were
full as fond of feafting as of fafting. Although this abbey is almoft literally diffolved, the fuperftitious effects of old
days infect the neighbourhood, for they
have faith in apparitions.

In our evening walk we paffed a man
who was driving his cart towards Bampton, and we afked him what names they
called thefe ftones * by, and how they
came there ?—He ftared, and afked
" What dun yaw want. t'kno for !"—
I dare fay this anfwer was occafioned
more by evening fears than by defigned
incivility: we had reafon to think fo, as
he was to go by a barn that has always
been the reputed haunt of ghofts †, and
which

* " The Devil's Stepping-Stones," by the country
people.

† " In the year 1759, a militia-man belonging to the
Weftmoreland corps, paffing near this haunted-houfe
(for,

which I believe is never passed in the day without a thought of them. Whilst we smile to hear such stories, let us not treat them with contempt, but rather regard them as the hereditary wanderings of honest minds that have not been sufficiently cultivated to disbelieve aërial NOTHINGS.

(for, the ignorant and credulous firmly at that time believed that the apparition of an old woman, clad in a long cloak, made her constant nocturnal perambulations near that place, to the no small terror of the bigoted passengers, fully persuaded of its reality), trod along with fear and trembling. When opposite the house, he had to pass along a stone wall, stretching from South to North near half a mile; he was unfortunately on the East side, and the moon shining very bright threw his shadow full against the wall, which he no sooner espied, than all the reports respecting the ghost seemed instantly verified. He ran till his limbs tottered under him and his martial spirit failed; but, luckily, at this momentous crisis, a gap in the wall allowed him to pass to the opposite side, and the old woman vanished. But the next morning he told such a tale of woe, that I am persuaded the stoutest grenadier in the whole corps durst not have gone the same road the succeeding night with a loaded musket and fixed bayonet.

The

The next morning I arofe with the hopes of getting a place in the mail-coach, as I had fent in the evening to Penrith to take one—it was full—and, as I could not *comprife* myfelf in the com-pafs of a letter, I grafped my fturdy hazle, as ftout a hazle as ever came out of Leven's woods, and which has always been more remarkable for producing large ones than any other, made my baggage a prefent of a ride, fhook my friend by the hand, and inftantly fet off.

I gave half an hour's contemplation to the Druids; and, in the confufion of ideas about their Cromlechs, Kiftvaens, and facred woods, a copy of verfes came into my head, that I wrote near a Pagan ruin in the Eaft Indies, and which I fhall infert after this chapter. But, as I have feen the laft lake, and have parted from the friend who was wont to cheer me when fatigued, and approve of my

6   defcrip-

defcriptions, I have only to fay that I reached Kendal after a folitary walk, whence, as I there commenced the Northern part of my ramble, I now take my departure.

ORIGINALLY

ᴏ̣ IGINALLY WRITTEN IN 1784, AT THE REQUEST
OF, AND AT THE BUNGALOW OF, LIEUT. S. W. NAN-
GREAVE, A RESIDENCE NEAR A PAGAN RUIN IN
BENGAL.

" It is not good for man to be alone ;"
Come, NANGREAVE ! let us make the world our own ;
In foft retirement tafte the learned page,
And live amidft the great of ev'ry age.
Immortal SHAKSPEARE ! muft unequall'd ftand,
The " fweeteft, wildeft," greateft, in the land ;
Father of thoughts ! that never had been known,
If Shakfpeare had not made fuch thoughts his own.
Old DRAYTON tells *whence* fprings and towns arofe,
Where beft the oak, *where* moft the poplar grows ;
His vigorous mind, and fcrutinizing eye,
No hill, no vale, no cuftom, paffes by.
Though his rough verfe fuits not the modern day,
Knowledge explains, and Fancy ftrews the way.
From SPENSER's fairy verfes learn to fcan
The various paffions in the mind of man ;
'Midft flowers and breaks the great Protector leads,
Hope flits aloft, and facred Truth fucceeds ;
As he will teach the true poetic ftrain,
Take penfive SHENSTONE, and with him complain ;
Or *Hagley's* Lord, who never penn'd a thought
" A dying man could ever wifh to blot."

De-

Defcriptive THOMSON, and kind Nature view,
With love-lorn HAMMOND, and wild COWLEY too,
Soft flowing WALLER richly wrote to pleafe,
And pointed SWIFT, with laughter-loving eafe.
Informing POPE, in varied greatnefs dreft,
By fweeteft numbers fooths the glowing breaft.
Take heaven-taught MILTON !—meditative YOUNG,
And fly with DRYDEN in his rapid fong.
More from correctnefs than poetic flame,
PRIOR ftands high in the great roll of fame.
Take melting MASON—elegiac GRAY,
And "catch the manners" from the gentle GAY.
Read roving LEE, tumultuoufly refin'd,
Who wrote with fuch ftrong energy of mind.
Emphatic OTWAY ! whom the great difown,
The Mufe's favourite, (but the Mufe alone !)
For SAVAGE mourn, and with his writings glow ;
His birth, his life, his death, were full of woe.

Rich-minded CAMOENS, Lufitania's boaft,
Tells all the dangers of the Cape's rough coaft ;
Of toils he fhar'd—of Eaftern battles won,
MICKLE tranflates, and makes the theme his own.
In one grand fcene—thus the great VASCO * faid,
" Why ftand appall'd, of what are ye afraid ?
" Do not ye fee the agitated main
" Trembles beneath the world's dread Sovereign ?

* See the Lufiad.—The effects of an earthquake off
the Cape of Good Hope.

Th'

Th' affrighted failors, by their leader cheer'd,
Hauld taut the ropes, the helmfman truly fteer'd;
The flutt'ring veffel felt the faving fails,
And rode triumphant 'midft the rougheft gales.
More able feamen Ocean never knew,
(Britons afide) than GAMA * and his crew.
With lucklefs FALCONER too fcud o'er the deep,
Weep o'er the tale, and for his mem'ry weep.
In numbers equal, though not in defign,
Tranflating BROOME with carelefs FENTON join.
Take HUDIBRAS, the lafher of his time,
Whofe fterling verfe appears in doggrel rhyme.
Laugh with gay STERNE in genuine language great,
Thoughtlefs, yet bleft with fentiment and wit.
BUDGELL, on whom the Nine with pleafure fmil'd,
In life's young ftage—the fleeting hours beguil'd;
But, older grown, the Being rafhly dar'd
To rufh from fcenes that made him unprepar'd.
Who more than ADDISON the age improv'd?
Who more refpected, or who more belov'd?
'Midft ftings from Critics, true to Virtue's caufe,
BLACKMORE wrote well, but feldom with applaufe.
And PHILIPS too, who left fo fmall a ftore,
We tafte his cider, and then wifh for more.
Mild mitred HURD, high ftation'd 'midft the beft,
With ev'ry virtue that adorns a breaft.
Take modern COWLEY, crown'd with living bays,
The firft of Fancy's children in our days.

* See the Lufiad.

U   Maternal

Maternal SMITH fo turns the poet's part,
Her matchlefs fonnets trill the feeling heart.
(Not like the vot'ries of a figh and tear,
That in foft numbers play about the ear.)
And with a Mufe of mind a SEWARD writes,
At once inftructing, and at once delights.
BARBAULD, though laft, not leaft that tune the ly e,
With ftrength of judgement and poetic fire.
With fuch—and more, of whom the fex may boaft,
Love them, aye love them, and applaud them moft.
In fweet retirement make all thefe your own,
'Tis thus, my friend, man never is alone,

ON

On RETIREMENT.

Hail, fweet Retirement! Meditation, hail!
On mountain high, or in refponfive vale;
Where no rude voice o'er pours the varied fong,
While Echo trembles to the tuneful throng;
Or by a rivulet's pellucid fide,
Where the calm hours in peaceful loit'rings glide;
Or near fome monument of Pagan fame,
Like yon in ruins, though unknown the name;
Where the cloath'd walls in mould'ring fragments lie,
And ftrike with grandeur the attentive eye;
     Hail, fweet Retirement!

When early fongfters, on melodious fpray,
Salute the op'ning fplendour of the day;
When the bright Sun bepurples the rich Eaft,
Or fets majeftic in the golden Weft;
And when protected from the noon-tide heat,
Beneath the umbrage of fome dun retreat;
Or, when the moon expels the womb of night,
Or fhine the ftars innumerably bright;
Frankly our inmoft thoughts we would unbend,
With thee, my firft companion, and my friend,
     In fweet Retirement!

                       Oh!

Oh ! that the waning years of life could be,
Near the fam'd town that bleſt our infancy ;
Where firſt a Soldier's life our fancy caught,
And fill'd the breaſt with manlineſs of thought;
Yet, if not there, on Britain's envy'd ſhore ;
How we would talk our martial ſtories o'er !
And if each had a lov'd and loving wife,
Thoſe dear ſolacers of declining life ;
How pleaſant to retrace paſt periods o'er,
And retroſpect what well we knew before,
    In ſweet Retirement !

F I N I S.

Errata.

Page 287, line 13, *for* " where," *read* " whence."